The Mission

Visit a planet, which the inhabitants abandoned. Determine where they went and if they will come to Earth.

What if the inhabitants never left?

What if they don't want visitors?

Landon, Inez and Chico

Landon intends to communicate with the Tititri if they are still alive. They hold the key to saving his daughter.

Inez intends to study them and their civilization.

Chico, if necessary, intends to kill them.

Enjoy the Two Previous Books In the Centauri Series

The Signal: They were coming, and they were not friendly

Prelude to Proxima: He had to save his ex-wife, his daughter and the entire planet

Available as e-books from Amazon, Barnes & Noble, iBooks and Kobo as well as in trade paper format.

Shorter Works by Rebecca S. W. Bates

Sharing Sol: Three short stories in the backstory world of the Centauri Series

The Time Is Light: Three stories about distortions in space and time

Tough Mothers: Three stories about the unique challenges of mothering in space

All available as e-books from Amazon, iBooks, Kobo, Barnes & Noble and other e-readers.

Sphinx of Centaurus

Rebecca S. W. Bates

D. M. Kreg Publishing

DMKregPublishing.com

For Emily, who carries the dream.

Acknowledgments

Thanks to the many writers who helped with this project, including the Northern Colorado Writers Workshop, and especially to Ed Bryant. Thanks also to the Inklings and the Oregon Writers Network. The mission to Centauri couldn't go without their keen insights and awesome support. Thanks to my professors at the University of Colorado who helped guide me with the science. Any errors are mine. Special thanks to my family for enduring my disruptions to our vacations and for believing in me. Thanks also to Donald Kreg, editor and publisher extraordinaire.

Sphinx of Centaurus

Rebecca S. W. Bates

Prologue

Pitch black darkness surrounded her. She was floating. Drifting. Through the dark.

Something sparked. Flickers of evanescence fluttered around her. She felt tickles. Smelled ozone. Awareness seeped through her, cell by cell.

Cold...

She felt...not numb but cold... It pierced her, deep enough that her core ached. The darkness that enfolded her was a sea of ice.

It is time, said a voice sliding out of the dark, resonating along the wires that connected her to the cryo-tank.

Cognizance flowed back. Her eyes blinked open to the dim interior of the *Centaurus*, the ship that carried her and the rest of this crew of seven. It carried the child host, too. All of them slept in frozen stasis while instruments guided their ship from Earth to Proxima Centauri.

Halfway out, it was time for a routine awakening, so that a human could make decisions to approve or reject the course corrections the ship had made while they slept.

Not quite human.

The parasite stirred within her.

Awake... Soon, she would be ready to follow its bidding and do what had to be done. She would use the Titinha to find the nexus, and then... She would destroy her.

Chapter One

Light seared into Landon Walker. Sterile, white light pulsed with blinking, red dots of charts and graphs. It had been less than two hours since his awakening in the cryo-tank, and his eyes still watered from the glare here aboard the *Centaurus*.

He massaged the stiffness from his back and bent closer to his daughter's tank. Its window showed him swirling clouds of frost and chemicals that suspended Molly, his baby girl. She looked so tiny in there. But then, at two years old she only filled about a third of its coffin-like interior. She was the only one still in suspension after the crew of seven had been awakened. The ship had reached its destination and inserted itself into orbit around Proxima's previously unknown, other planet.

He shivered. Doc kept the cryogenics bay of the *Centaurus* uncomfortably cold as long as it held any occupants. But it wasn't just the ship that felt cold. Doc had told him it was normal to continue feeling chilled long after cryo-sleep. Maybe several more hours, or even days. He'd scarcely awakened in his own tank when he'd started calling out for his daughter. Finally, he'd recovered enough strength to wobble over here and personally check on her.

"There, you see?" Doc said at his side. She was a bald woman with a sharp face and a pinched nose, and she insisted that everyone call her "Doc" instead of her real name, Renee

Montague. She clasped his arm, keeping him from falling as he leaned over Molly's tank. "Everything is normal, just as I told you." Besides a nasal twang, she spoke with an accent that swallowed her words. "She is fine, as fine as a sleeping toddler can be. You believe me now, yes?"

He'd never doubted Doc. She was the best medical specialist that the field of cryogenic suspension had to offer. No, it wasn't Doc whom he questioned. Nor his own normal chills.

It was Molly.

He had to be sure the alien hadn't hurt her.

Because Doc wouldn't know about that. No one on this ship knew about the duality, except for him. And Greer, his sister. But they'd left her behind on Earth.

"All right, you've seen her," Doc said, tugging on his sleeve. "Now we take care of *you*. You still need a little more time coming out."

Resisting her effort to pull him away, he squinted at the window. Through the fog that wrapped around the delicate features of his daughter's face, he could make out glimpses of her closed eyes. She slept, peacefully.

He remembered the way the alien had ridden her back on Earth. Another face had tumbled into view under his daughter's flesh, glowing through her skin like the message inside an antique eight ball. Each time the alien had surfaced from within her, it changed the color of Molly's eyes from golden brown to emerald green. The face had looked like an adult, human woman's.

It wasn't.

Doc kept tugging. "You always get your way, yes? What I don't understand is how you managed to convince the bosses to allow you to bring her along with us."

"It's a long story," he said. He'd vowed never to leave his daughter's side again, and Sam and the other bosses had wanted him badly enough to agree to his terms.

At least Molly looked the same as when he himself had gently laid her here all those years ago back at the space launch platform orbiting Earth. They'd barely escaped Patagonia with their lives intact. Molly's mother hadn't. They'd had to leave Summer there, buried under the ice of a glacier, but had he and Molly really escaped anything? His daughter lay encased in frozen sleep, while her mother also lay frozen, although not in sleep, more than four light years away. And the alien... It was contained for now, as long as his daughter slept.

He blinked away the fuzz of teary vision. Molly looked the same, but... There was something odd about the fog of chemicals swirling around her. A ribbon of empty space, no wider than the blade of a knife, parted the fog above her face.

His legs gave out, but Doc caught him before he fell. "Be careful. You think my post-cryonic drugs work your system like a miracle? I will help you to the washroom. But no shaving yet, yes? Not until after you regain your steadiness."

She steered him across the laboratory, outfitted around a ring of eight cryo-tanks—seven of them empty—and deposited him on a bench inside the small cubicle of facilities. One new uniform hung from a hook. She pointed it out as his, and then closed the door as she left.

Steadiness may never come again, he thought while washing up. Not with the weight of what he alone knew. What he couldn't share. Because of Molly. It was all for her.

Even the signal.

They'd skimmed across galactic space, a bullet across a

gulf of time, chasing down an energy emission coming from the Centauri system, aimed at Earth. Landon had captured it with his tachyonic equipment, designed to collect faster-than-light particles, and then converted it to a recording, which he'd handed over to his bosses at the International Space Agency headquartered in the Brazilian state of Goiás. The directors in turn had passed along the recording to their Amazonian linguists who deciphered a message that warned of death, as in the end of time. Consequently, ISA had mounted this mission to gather information about what to expect, so they could take appropriate measures to counter the threat.

But the directors were wrong. It wasn't a message about death for Earth. It was the Centaurians who were dying. They were an ancient civilization who called themselves Tititri, and they needed Earth's help. Their leader, the Titinha, had told all this to Landon through Molly. The aliens intended to hold his baby daughter hostage through their crisis. Landon would make them release her if it was the last thing he ever did.

Sometime later he emerged from the washroom, fully dressed in his new jumpsuit uniform. The designers had put more effort into the new ISA logo for his sleeve, showing a bridge from Earth to the stars, than the more practical matters of comfort. The rough, gray-blue fabric itched his skin. Never mind that. They'd made it across the bridge of space to Earth's nearest star, Proxima Centauri. They were the first humans ever to cross the gulf of interstellar space.

And now he was clean-shaven.

Doc did a double take, and he winked. She lifted one finger and opened her mouth, but before she could scold him, a bell chimed.

"Damnation," she said. "I warned them not to sound the summons down here."

Her grumbling protests faded behind him as he hurried out.

2

Moving through the length of the ship, Landon felt as if lead weights were tied round his ankles. He was only fifty-one years old, or rather, that's what he had been before leaving Earth. He was the oldest one on this mission by a dozen years, but he shouldn't be too old to chase stars. And yet... This awakening left him feeling clumsier than he'd felt that other time, a lifetime ago, when he'd slept cryogenically to and from Titan, testing his tachyonic equipment, not expecting to find what they found. Alien ruins. And Summer, his wife, had inexplicably accessed his sperm bank during his absence, and Molly began to grow.

A burning ache of flaccid muscles worked too hard, too soon, spread through his body. It tired him just to think of the amount of work he would face if he ever wanted to regain his martial arts control. For a fleeting moment, he wondered why, given his insignificance in the universe, should he try? Why did it matter if he'd slipped?

He shoved the doubt from his mind, as quickly as it had appeared. The answer was simply survival. There was no other choice, not if he planned to survive. He would find the necessary discipline, because he had to.

At the end of the rotating midship, he plunged into the connector to the fixed foreship and felt the disquieting shift of his organs as he swam awkwardly from artificial gravity toward weightlessness. Thanks to Dr. Montague and her cautious administration of post-cryonic drugs, he would be well behind the others responding to the summons bell. He tried to make up for his tardiness by moving too fast, and he bumped his forehead against the opening to the laboratory level, thudding dangerously close to the humming instruments.

Ruy Schulz, the planetary geologist who doubled as a xeno-geoarcheologist, fussed over his readings, so absorbed in his work that he didn't seem to notice Landon's clumsy entrance.

With one hand Landon grappled for a handlebar to stop his wild movement, and with the other he rubbed his head where the bump already welled. "You know what this summons is all about?"

Ruy looked up from his scope. His motion swung two foot-long braids around him like flailing whips. With gravity, his sandy hair fell over his ears, but here in the weightlessness of the science lab, the tails looked like electrified prongs standing straight out. From the Netherlands, he seemed as ill-suited to playing astronaut as Landon felt, but the brilliance of Ruy's resume—he'd contributed to the massive project of reclaiming Dutch territory from rising seas, among other things—had won him a seat on the mission to Proxima.

Ruy nodded. "Commander Masambwa wants us to pool what we've learned so far about the object—"

"Object?" Landon was still trying to understand how intelligent life could've evolved on an unknown planet orbiting a red dwarf in a triple star system.

Ruy went on. "It's a massive object on the surface of this planet, which we did not even know existed. It remained hidden from us, in the shadow of its sister—"

"Orbital dynamics are not shadows." A wave of dizziness hit Landon.

Ruy shrugged. "Anyway, the commander thinks maybe this object is the source of the emission, since your tracking device led us here while we were all still in cryostasis. I tried to tell her that we don't have enough information yet to make that hypothesis, but she won't listen to me."

"Is it a land formation, or something the Tititri built?" Or someone else? Maybe the Tititri had come here from somewhere else.

Ruy turned back to his instrument, speaking to its blinking lights. "That's the question, isn't it? We've seen some evidence of uplifting, but we're unsure if this object is natural or not."

"Uplifting? You mean it's a volcano?"

"No, there's no vulcanism. At least, not anymore."

"You must have some ideas what it is."

Ruy frowned at the graphs displaying before him. "I can form no assumptions about the object until I learn more about the planet. The presence of mountains suggests that this planet was geologically active at some point in its history. However, that may be a hasty assessment. There's no magnetic field, no liquid core, no convection. Very thin atmosphere. Nothing apparently going on beneath the surface. In fact, with the low average density, it appears that there's nothing at all beneath the surface."

Landon took a deep breath to steady himself. "What are you saying? This is an artificial world?"

"I am not prepared to make such an assessment, not yet."

"But you're saying it isn't a planet?" Landon always felt frustrated by the geologist's evasiveness. Nothing had changed from their training days together at ISA headquarters in Goiás.

"It's not so simple," Ruy said with a sigh. "There's a thin ring

19

in orbit around this alleged planet, suggesting it might've had a moon at one time. In any case, whether it's a planet or even something less than that, we should see other planetesimals, the leftovers from planetary formation. Where are they? Maybe they're yet to be found, but so far, we haven't spotted a single one. Did they all blow away in the T Tauri winds? Margot will have to answer that one for us at the briefing."

The solar astronomer, Landon thought, would be equally irritated with impatience over delays. He pushed off from his handlebar, but Ruy didn't release from the grippers that held him in place before his instruments. "Aren't you coming?"

"In a minute. But before you go, there's something else you should know."

Landon thudded against the doorway leading to the flight deck and groped for something to cling to. "Yeah? What?"

"I shouldn't be the one to tell you this, but you'd better be prepared. You see, it happened while we were all in suspension, on our way out here from Earth. When we were negotiating through the Oort Cloud of Sol's system. While the ship was running on its pre-set program and the scanners were watching out for us, so they could make the necessary adjustments."

"Yeah, and?" In a way, it comforted Landon to realize that nothing had changed as a result of cryonic suspension. The Dutchman still could never get to his point. "*What* happened?"

Ruy went on, even more slowly. "Ship's scanners picked up a trail of electromagnetic radiation streaming from the general direction of the Milky Way's core. It was similar to the X-ray emissions that come from accretion disks around black holes."

The hesitation in his cautious voice sent a shudder down Landon's spine, and it had nothing to do with the chills from his recent recovery from cryogenics.

"What's odd," Ruy said, "is that these X-rays are interspersed with visible light."

"What are you saying? Was there an image attached to it, like the one we picked up before? Back on Earth?"

"No, it's not that simple. I'm afraid I have some bad news to tell you, as a result of all this. The emission from the galactic core disrupted our tachyonic communications with Earth while we were in transit."

"So you're saying the system went down?" Landon drifted away from the door as he swiped the back of his head with its flattened bristles of hair. His voice growled. "How long was it down?"

"Um, it still is. That is, as far as Earth is concerned." Ruy looked away from him, back to his instruments.

"Earth doesn't know that we've arrived here?"

"Well, not yet. They'll know about our arrival in another four and a quarter more years. We've been exchanging radio signals, you see."

"Then, I've got plenty of work to do, getting everything back online. We've got to make contact with Earth sooner than that." Landon twisted around, aiming for the exit. "Why didn't Masambwa have me awakened as soon as the problem was detected?"

"Your name wasn't on the duty roster, and Chico's was."

"But he's the pilot."

"He trained on your instruments."

"Only as backup. He can't fix them as well as I can."

"No," Ruy said, "but he can maneuver the ship in an emergency. Can you? Anyway, they found that your entire tachyonic set-up had malfunctioned, apparently as a result of the galactic core emission, so Chico disconnected it."

"He *what*?" Landon trembled as rage steamed through him, seeking a vent. He wanted to protest the lost work, the months of alignment he'd put into his equipment, only to have it all undone by...a hotshot pilot. But he kept his mouth shut, knowing that whatever slipped out now would be words he'd regret later.

"Apparently, there was some thought that you might disapprove," Ruy said. "At first, Chico tried to restore the tachcom himself, but when he couldn't—"

"They could've awakened me then. I could've fixed it."

"Of course you could," Ruy said soothingly. "What I'm trying to tell you is that since the system was down anyway, he ended up borrowing pieces of it for enhancing the images of the planet. Masambwa's orders."

Landon erupted inside, a collision of frustration, impatience, and fear. What the hell was going on here? Didn't they understand their urgent situation? The ever-present threat of death? Not just the Tititri's, but theirs as well. But all he let show was a single twitch of one finger, slipping from his grip on the edge of the doorway.

"Why didn't she wake me up then, to at least consult me?" His voice cracked. "It's *my* equipment."

"Of course it is," Ruy said, smoothing the ruffled air with his hands. "You know how the commander is. She rules this ship with iron fists. What she wants, she gets. She wanted a particular image of the planet, and your equipment comes with the best sensor on the ship for zeroing in on target areas."

Landon suppressed the twitches that rocketed through him.

"Okay. I'll get to work re-setting everything."

"Not yet. Your equipment is still presently unavailable, as long as they're enhancing that montage of the site surrounding the object. You'll have to wait until it's done."

"But—"

"Recall that our equipment must serve double duty whenever possible. You understand?"

Landon scowled. A throb pulsed at the back of his head as Ruy patiently went on, explaining about their need to conserve space and resources. In case Landon hadn't gotten it.

He had. Did Ruy think he was the type who could disregard procedure?

Finally, the geologist summed up. "Besides, with a four-plus-year lag in radio communication with Earth, the general public has probably already forgotten about us by now, or at least they would fear we're lost. It'll be another four years before they learn any different."

What Ruy really meant, Landon thought, swallowing hard to suppress his irritation, was that the general public didn't understand his tachcom. Even the scientific community lacked confidence. He admitted that his device looked unwieldy with its multiple parts—scoops and screens, coils and cables, dishes and tubes of chemicals—and all of them hooked together, looking like a backyard science experiment gone viral. But it worked. It communicated nearly instantaneously via captured tachyons, no easy accomplishment in itself. No one else had his particular touch with the instruments, except for Van Pelt, who had far exceeded Landon's work. Either skeptics or aliens had driven that researcher mad, and he'd ending up hanging himself. A fate Landon didn't wish for himself.

He nodded and said, "How long do they need?"

"We won't know until we pass over the area again in another..." Ruy's gaze shifted to the timescreen above the door. "...Thirty-five minutes. That's when we can take a closer look at this object, and after that, you can realign your tachcom."

3

Landon didn't wait well, strapped into the seat at the imager, next station over from his own console and its disassembled parts. Stripped tubes, empty casings, and leftover coils clipped into holders, surrounding him like a broken net of assorted parts. There wasn't much he could do, other than watch the images that sprang to life on the viewscreen before him. Two of his crewmates—Commander Masambwa and Margot Brandt, the solar astronomer—strapped into their workstations at the front of the cylinder-shaped flight deck, while two others floated in freefall from the far end, moving this way. They were drawn, no doubt, to the projected view on his screen.

Shadowy surface features of the planet below formed and dissolved before him, and then reformed into shapes. Craters, dead volcanoes and weblike gouges marred otherwise barren plains.

The planet appeared Mars-like. Dead.

But it must've lived at some point in the past. The Tititri had sent their warning signal from here. Something had threatened their planet and had left it like this. That much his crewmates knew.

They didn't know the rest of it, that Landon had found the remains of their scoutship in Patagonia.

Whatever had killed the planet had caused the Tititri to flee, looking for a new home. He wondered why they hadn't gone to their sister planet. Even if it hadn't been livable, he assumed terraforming would've been easier than leaving their solar system. Why had they sought Earth instead? He couldn't discuss these issues with his crewmates. He couldn't reveal what he knew, not if he held any hopes for bringing Molly safely through her ordeal.

The Tititri had sworn him to secrecy. They needed Molly to activate their final integration on Earth, although why they'd chosen her, he wasn't sure. It was most likely because of Summer. So many questions had died with Molly's mother under the glacier of Patagonia. In any case, Molly's role in the alien invasion wouldn't happen until she grew to adult size. At least, that's what the Titinha had assured him when speaking through Molly.

Cryogenic sleep would delay the aliens' plans.

Landon had scored a small victory by negotiating with Sam and his other bosses on Earth to bring Molly along in cryostasis. The mission needed him to work his equipment, and two seats had become available on the *Centaurus*, following the accident he'd escaped in the Amazonian jungle. But Landon feared that his victory would be short-lived. He couldn't keep Molly in suspension indefinitely. And then what?

Something had killed this planet, and that something could threaten Earth, too. The Tititri had tried to warn them.

As the surface features defined themselves more sharply, his drifting crewmates jostled against the back of his chair, angling for a better view. They murmured and bantered in his ears.

A finger reached past his cheek and pointed at the screen.

25

"Here it comes again," said Inez Pereira, the Brazilian linguist-slash-pilot on the mission. The rising star. The new recruit from the slums of Rio. Look how far she'd come.

She leaned low, bringing her cheek next to his. "That object is coming back into view." Her face glowed shiny clean, scrubbed fastidiously, almost raw. Kinky, coal-black hair pulled back into a tight tail. Its ends tickled the back of his neck. A necklace swung loose from her collar, and its nugget-sized charm bumped against his shoulder.

"Dr. Walker." Masambwa's no-nonsense, formal voice thundered across the flight deck from her command station. "Magnify this sector. Do it now. I want more details."

"Yes, ma'am."

Inez withdrew from Landon's shoulder. Everyone fell silent as he brought up the images. He felt Masambwa's steel gaze pierce the air, and he summoned strength of will into his fingers, rat-tat-tatting them across the touchscreen.

Masambwa broke the pattern of thumping sounds with a grunt. "Captain Pereira, you will be in charge of the landing party, and as such you will report to me. Thoughts?"

Inez, still hovering behind Landon, responded in a hushed voice, filled with wonder. "I'd like to set up base camp as close to the object as possible."

"How close?"

Chico drifted over. "You want me to land the shuttlecraft on top of the object?"

"Hardly, Lieutenant," Masambwa said as if the pilot's wisecrack had been serious. "It's an unsuitable land formation."

"I don't like the looks of those plains." Chico reached past Landon's shoulder and stabbed at a smooth, dark area surrounding the unresolved object in question.

"Right," Inez said from Landon's other side. "Too unstable. It's a sea of sand."

"Wrong." Chico argued back, with Landon caught in the middle. "They're too open. We need to take up a defensive position, for when the aliens attack. The shuttlecraft has enough fire power built into its gunwales to blow that object into a pile of pulverized sand."

Inez reached across Landon and patted Chico's arm. "Calm down, that won't happen. No one's going to attack. The Tititri are long gone. Take a look. Do you see any evidence that could support life?"

Chico snorted. "That's what the enemy wants you to think. Trust me, they're there."

"Where?"

"Inside the object, I'd bet."

Masambwa cut them off. "Lieutenant, do you have privileged information?"

"No more than what the rest of us have, ma'am. Captain Pereira translated the message, so she should know. 'You die next,' that's what it said. And I say: not if I can help it. Ma'am."

Inez said, "They were evacuating their world because of something killing them off, and they were warning us that we face the same danger on Earth."

Landon choked. His muscles twisted into knots. She'd guessed the Tititri's purpose, while most of those privileged few at ISA who knew about the alien message assumed it was a battle cry. If she guessed any more—that they *weren't* gone, that they planned to migrate to Earth—then the Tititri would think he'd told her, perhaps to thwart their plans. And then what would they do to Molly? Now that the *Centaurus* was here? It was too late to turn back.

Chico scoffed. "You can't know what aliens intend. Look at what happened to Landon's ex-wife. She thought she knew all about those aliens, and a lot of good it did her." He slashed one finger across his throat.

Landon prickled all over and clenched his fist. "That has nothing to do with this."

"From context," Inez said, "there are clues, and I'm telling you, they weren't personally threatening us."

"Not likely," Chico said. "We have to be prepared for attack."

Masambwa interrupted. "Lieutenant Torres is correct. The landing party needs to assume a defensive position."

Landon couldn't let them make his job any harder to do. "If I'm going to assemble a remote terminal to track their trail," he said, "then I'm going to need to be close enough to haul my equipment over there."

"Duly noted." Inez pointed to the edge of the dark sea where a narrow strip of relatively smooth terrain lay at the base of a mountain range. "What about this area? Chico, do you think you could put us down here?"

"Whatever you say."

"Wait." Masambwa's single word sounded like a hammer. "Go back."

Landon scrolled through the captured images until she told him where to stop. The quibbling on the flight deck faded away as he adjusted the magnification of one area of the unknown object. Maybe it was the source of the emission...

Voices at the far end of the cylinder announced the arrival of Doc and Ruy. Masambwa looked up, and the scowl on her face read: *It's about time you decided to join us.*

"I wonder what it is?" Inez whispered, staring at the screen.

"Rock formations," Chico said.

Landon studied the image of the massive land formation and sharpened the contrast, defining the image before them. One end of the object protruded up, apparently as tall as the object was long.

Inez gasped. "Is that...a head? It is! And look, there's a face on it, too. See those circles? They're eyes."

Landon stared at the image of a human head tilting up from a blocky shape, as if staring up into the emptiness of space. As if it watched them, orbiting above.

No, not a *human* head.

"Explanations?" Masambwa said.

Doc squeezed between them and peered at the screen. "It could be a trick of light and shadow. An optical illusion."

Inez's voice dropped low. "Look. I thought at first it was human, but it isn't really human at all. The jaw is too long. It's almost...simian."

Doc laughed. "I will tell you. It is more like Neanderthal Man. In fact, it almost looks like a professor I once had. In a class on evolution."

Inez leaned over the back of Landon's chair and peered closer at the screen. "It's a sphinx," she said. "The Tititri built a sphinx."

Masambwa raised her voice. "All right, people. That's enough. Back to work. Move."

Inez and Chico tumbled away. Landon lifted his eyes from the image before him and studied the timescreen. They were moving out of range already. They had their montage. He tapped in instructions to store the recordings, shut down the imager, and transfer the sensor to his tachyonic equipment at the neighboring station. Then he unstrapped and floated over, ready to realign the tachcom. Soon, they would be talking to Earth.

Except... After unclipping miscellaneous parts, reassembling them, running tests, shutting down the system, taking its pieces apart and starting all over again, he discovered that his equipment hadn't simply malfunctioned. The problem went deeper. A hidden code had been entered into its program.

Someone or some*thing* had deliberately tampered with his equipment.

Chapter Two

Landon's stomach lurched as the shuttlecraft dipped closer to the frozen surface of the planet. He'd felt unsettled, almost ill, ever since his discovery aboard the orbiter. Who would've wanted to sabotage his tachcom?

He'd reported it to Masambwa who'd demanded repairs and promised to find the culprit. But how could she? He kept wondering all the while as he'd reassembled parts and restored his original settings. And then he'd sent a message to Earth, although no response had been received by the time the launch window came to shuttle down here. With one last glance at Molly, sleeping in her tank—would he ever see her again?— he'd boarded the shuttlecraft. Now, this landing didn't help the matter of his queasiness.

Night had already fallen on the surface as they zeroed in on their landing spot. The lights from their vehicle swept through the dark and illuminated a half-circle of totem-like boulders below. His breath caught in his throat as the craft shuddered, rocked, and eased down closer to the broken henge structure. Tickles crept across his flesh, squeezing beneath the tight layer of his spacesuit liner.

This arrangement of rocks seemed as deliberate as the head they'd seen from orbit.

These rocks were no act of nature. Something had broken them, too.

Sabotaging his equipment was the same as subverting the mission. It could've happened anywhere between Goiás and here, by anyone from tech support to *Centaurus* crew. He glanced around at his four crewmates, strapped into their seats in the bean-pod style craft—Ruy, Doc, Inez, and Chico. Was it one of them? Or one of the two who remained behind on the orbiter—Margot and Masambwa.

He shuddered, almost wishing that the saboteur could be an alien instead, someone with more advanced technology than theirs, someone who'd known how to access the ship. Ruy had told him about a disruption from the galactic core. Maybe it had happened then. He didn't know.

He'd handed the problem over to Masambwa, but he couldn't let go of it entirely.

"Touchdown," Chico said from the pilot's seat. Cheers arose inside their craft and over the com, from the ship orbiting above, 23,000 kilometers away.

Where Molly remained. Asleep, in frozen stasis.

Buckles clicked and released around him. Straps flung softly aside in the one-third Earth gravity. Ruy, Doc, and Inez lurched from their seats to embrace each other and slap Chico on the back. The pilot ate up their attention, and Landon rolled his eyes. Chico had only been doing his job, same as everyone else. They would have ninety days to get the job done on the surface of the planet before their food and water supplies required their return.

Would Masambwa have answers for him by then?

None of them could wait to get out there onto the surface, in spite of the night. There was no reason to wait for dawn, since daylight under a red dwarf star at this distance wouldn't be bright enough to work without extra lighting, anyway. Still, there was procedure to follow. Crates of equipment to unload.

Finally, Landon's turn came. But when the shuttle's airlock door whooshed open, and he took his first steps onto the regolith of an extrasolar world, words to describe this momentous event evaporated from his mind. The sharp intake of his breath rasped through the mouthpiece of his pressurized suit. His feet froze in place. His gaze glued to the star dome.

They were the first human star travelers to escape the solar system.

Silvery light from billions of stars struck the narrow ring that arced overhead and bathed the plains before them. Scoured by eons of winds, the planet's surface rippled toward distant peaks that rose like ninja shadows.

Then a generator thrummed to life, and voices crowded through his link. Floodlights flared bright, dispelling the night and its sense of wonder. Whatever it was that had chilled him, vanished with the appearance of light. He chin bumped the corder, turning it on to record all that he saw into his suit's memory. Then he lifted his bin of equipment, crammed full of the parts he would need to build a remote terminal for his tachcom, and set off. The lighter gravity put a lightness to his step as he followed Inez, captain of the landing party, across the crunchy regolith. Alien soil.

Two of the crew were already outside, springing easily in the light gravity as they unloaded crates of equipment. The rover had come off first, and now the short distance from the shuttlecraft to the rover looked like an obstacle course with crates of building materials littering the way.

Landon stumbled. Dismayed, he wondered how long it

would take to regain the strength that cryogenics had stolen from him. As far as he knew, none of the research labs had ever tested any subjects for as long as the *Centaurus* crew had been frozen.

And then there was Molly. By the time they returned to Earth, several decades would have passed there, but physically she would still be a child of two. What about Greer? What would his frivolous sister have become by then? One never knew, where Greer was concerned. No, he and Molly would be on their own. Assuming Earth survived the alien invasion—and he had to remain positive and believe it would—would he ever regain his life that had been so disrupted by these Tititri?

"Landon," Inez called over the link, interrupting his attempt to grasp meaning from a situation beyond meaning. "You can trade places with one of the construction team, if you prefer to stay behind." She was already at the rover, waiting for him. Watching him. Evaluating him.

He chinned on his short-range communicator. "No, ma'am. Let's go." His boots crunched the frozen granules as he cautiously made his way around the crates toward the rover.

He hauled himself and the bin up, over the balloon tires to the rover's hatch. Inez sealed it behind them. Air hissed in, and neither of them spoke while the airlock pressurized. The vacuum brushbot moved over them, removing dust, then the inner door slid open into the cab. Flicking off the corder, he and Inez removed their helmets, conserving their suits' precious supplies of oxygen. Landon inhaled a faint taste of iron as they ducked inside.

He stowed his helmet on the rack above the suit renewer, then squeezed past two bench seats and into the driver's armchair.

Inez strapped herself into the navigator's seat beside him and nodded approval to power up the drive. The vehicle came to life with a soft hum of the engine and the oily smells from its freshly lubricated parts. The box-shaped supraluminal particle sensor, which would track the trail of the emission, sat between him and Inez. She swung around in her seat and switched on its audio portion. No pulsating "ping" sounded. The aliens' signal was dead, Landon thought, just like their planet. Dread swirled through him, knotting his insides. He felt certain that the Tititri intelligence was preserved somewhere on their home world, and he meant to find it. Somehow, he would convince them to release their control over Molly *now*. He had no intentions of cooperating with them by waiting until his daughter reached maturity.

Hastily, he spun the rover around. They wove past the totem-like boulders of a semicircular formation only a hundred feet or so away from their landing site. Half a dozen boulders remained upright, standing tall in the footprint of a henge. At least twice as many had collapsed, splayed onto their sides. The debris of smaller, broken pieces sprinkled around the entire structure, toppled over in the wind. The rover was like a bug, trying to find a path through a playing field of a child's spilled blocks.

Once they'd negotiated past the henge and its boulders, they emerged from the shadow of jagged mountains. They headed due east and rocked from side to side as the vehicle dipped down slowly onto the sea of sand. Straight ahead lay the curved line of an empty horizon where sandy plains met a dark sky. Not space, but a thin atmosphere. This sky would see dawn in three more hours.

"Why do you think they built that head over there?" Inez asked, breaking the spell that held them in silent awe.

It seemed like such a long time ago when he'd been skeptical about the presence of other intelligent life in the universe. Now, his beliefs had turned upside down. He couldn't be sure about anything. "Hard to tell."

She laughed. "We saw that head so clearly from orbit. And its face. Makes you wonder about its purpose."

"Right." *It's where they are.*

They drove on in silence, lurching over smaller bits of rock litter mixed into the sand. The only sounds came from the thrum of the battery-powered engine, until Inez finally spoke again.

"Do you think you can find the exact source of the emission even without the signal?" Her voice vibrated from the monotonous hum.

"With the SLP sensor we can."

"But is it going to work?" She nodded at the silent device sitting between them.

"It works, don't worry. We did plenty of testing on it in my labs, long before I came on board to this project. It proved reliable then. And besides, it led us to this planet once we entered the periphery of the Centauri system. It won't fail now."

"I know, but the fact is that the ship's tachcom failed."

"That's fixed now."

"But is it fully functional? It didn't seem to work when you sent your message before we came down here."

"It works." He regretted the harshness of his voice, but okay, he admitted he was a bit sensitive to criticism. Hell, it was his life's work. Then, in a softer voice, he continued. "Everything

36

is re-set. We've never tested it at this great of a distance before. There must be a lag time..."

"Ah, so you *do* have doubts." Against the faint green light emitting from the dashboard of instruments, he could barely make out her grin. She was teasing him.

He grunted. She didn't need to know the bloody details of his many failures. Only one of them really mattered in the end: Molly. He squeezed the controls tighter, and the vehicle swerved around one end of a blocky-shaped boulder, swinging them against the straps of their seats.

Laughing, Inez reached into the neck of her suit, then pulled out the nugget-sized gold charm she always wore on a chain. "Where I come from, nothing is certain. That's why this *figa* is so important. It's a symbol of luck from the old ways."

"You really believe in that superstition?" he asked, glancing at the charm shaped like a tiny fist, with its thumb inserted between its index and middle fingers.

"My mother does. She gave me this *figa*. She felt I'd need something extra on this mission. That science and technology weren't enough."

"Huh." The tone of his huff made his opinion clear. She turned away from him and stared out at the blackness. He softened his voice. "We're in charge of our own destiny. That's all I meant."

Inez sighed. "I'm not so quick to deny the unexplainable. Besides, making contact is the dream of all humanity."

He already had. But he couldn't tell her about it, so he bit his tongue and steered the rover through waves of sand. Beyond the cone of illumination from the rover's headlights appeared a wall of darkness, as dark as that cavern on Earth where he'd found them. They'd sworn him to secrecy, promising to release Molly only if he kept the knowledge of their presence on Earth secret. Molly's life depended on his bargain with the aliens.

"They've been here and gone," Inez said. "We'll get plenty of evidence of them on this mission. It's only a question of time. But we have to be careful. Now that you say you've got the tachcom up and running again on the ship, we don't want to be premature with any announcements to the public that might send them into a panic about a planet killer on the loose. You and I know the truth. Those aliens warned us about the destruction in that signal they sent us, because it's heading to Earth."

His fingers tightened on the controls, and the rover lurched forward, swooshing sprays of sand past their windows. He wished he could be as certain as she seemed that the aliens were only trying to help Earth. "Can you be sure about your translation? What's your Rosetta stone? What could possibly be the connection between an alien language and one of your remote Amazonian languages?"

"That's what we're going to find out," she said, patting the boxy SLP sensor that sat in the space between them. She fell as silent as the device.

The hum of the engine vibrated through his body, tickling him. He stared ahead, following the reach of their headlights that pierced the unknown.

Finally, a loud sigh from Inez broke their rhythmic swishing through the sea of sand. "Assume for a moment that you wanted to leave a message for another race with whom you had no idea how to communicate. How would you do it? How would you communicate with someone that may not even use language as we know it?"

"You wouldn't. People who speak the same language can't even communicate."

"But that doesn't stop them from wanting to. Or trying. Don't you think it's reasonable that they would build an object and put it in the most unlikely place? With a signaling device on top of that, it becomes obvious and draws attention to itself. And it worked, didn't it? We picked up their signal from Earth, and it accomplished what it set out to do. It has drawn us here. It's the beginning of communication, you see? What's left is the rest of the tachyonic message to decipher. But that will come, too."

He felt light-headed, peering at the landscape before them. He drew in a sharp breath, and his hands slipped from the controls. The rover jerked to a stop. A shadow rose ahead, emerging from beyond the curved line of the horizon.

"There it is," she murmured.

His heart hammered against his chest, drumming a rhythmic pulse in his ears. Dread coursed through his body like a thick molasses.

"C'mon, let's go," she said.

He nodded and swallowed. The only sound between them was the whir of the rover's engine as they advanced on the rock formation, which grew larger and larger before them. Like a mesa, at home.

Closer and closer. The mesa loomed above them. Close enough that their headlights traced crevices in the walls. From this angle, the rocks *did* resemble a giant beast. The sphinx crouched on its haunches, as if ready to pounce, with its simian head tilted up toward space.

2

Lieutenant Chico Torres slouched against the shuttlecraft's viewport, facing east. He watched red smears across the horizon where Alpha, the biggest of the Centaurian stars, would soon rise at 5:00 Earth Standard Time. Commander Masambwa had imposed EST on the mission as their way to measure time, and he thought it typical of her to try to force an entire planet to conform. Never mind that the planet only had a twenty-hour rotation cycle. Did she think no one would miss 21:00 through 24:00? No one, that is, except for Chico, who lived for party time at night.

Signaling the end of night, the hint of color hovered above the general area where the sphinx formation lay, ten kilometers away and out of sight beyond the horizon. A faint glow of red touched the emptiness between here and there.

Ten hours here on the planet's surface since touchdown at dusk—now it was almost dawn—and already those empty plains were showing evidence of alien infestation. Tire tracks etched a road between here and there. *And we are the aliens*, he thought, waiting for the sunrise and feeling an emptiness in his gut. Inez and Landon were making history over there, while here on the shuttlecraft, Chico had been left behind to do finger exercises. Fucking odd that the bosses hadn't figured out a way to make him useful when they assigned him to com desk duty.

Must be pay-back.

For all the sunrises he'd seen from Mars, Earth, SpaceHab, and the Moon. Unofficially, not that he was counting, he held the International Space Agency's record for most sunrises shared with babes—

Shit.

He tried to remember not to call them that, especially not while he was on duty, if you could call this duty. He couldn't help it. He admitted it. He'd been born with superior genes that appreciated the fairer sex. He'd learned at an early age to conceal them as much as he could, because his attitude had landed him in trouble more times than he could count. It probably didn't matter anymore. He'd gotten the hell out of Port Lowell. It wasn't exactly a "port," being buried underground on Mars, and worst of all, no one there had fully appreciated his skills. He'd longed to get re-posted to something more daring, a place like Ceres, a place that would give him the fame and glory creds he deserved.

This wasn't Ceres, but in the long run, and man, did he mean the long run, this could turn out even better. No matter what the pussy-foot commander might tell them, he would be ready to shoot any aliens before they shot him. Why else was this craft loaded? He'd save them all, and then, once they returned to Earth System who knew how many years into his future, without aging more than a year at most, they'd finally shower him with the fame and glory he deserved, for having endured the shit of this voyage. Best of all, there'd be no Uncle Jota to undermine him anymore, unless the bastard was too mean to die of old age. Death was the only way the senate would get rid of him, too.

Chico cracked his knuckles and glanced over his shoulder at the equipment he was supposed to be monitoring. No red warning lights flashing. Nothing going on. Too bad. He was eager to shoot some aliens.

Pulling away from the imminent sunrise, he turned to the

west viewport, toward the site they'd selected to erect their base. It would become the International Space Agency's first permanent base outside the solar system, and Chico didn't even have the honor of constructing *that*.

No, instead the honor had gone to the two scientists, Ruy Schulz the geologist, and Renee Montague, their physician. Chico snorted. Pieces of equipment littered the virgin soil nearby. If only the duty roster called for him to have a piece of some of the important work, instead of manning the com desk, he'd show them how to get the job done.

At least the scientists had figured out how to inflate the two bubbles of base. He could see their lop-sided, egg-shaped, Siamese twin outlines under the floodlights.

Chico smacked one fist against the palm of his other hand. Sure, com desk duty was important, too. Someone had to be here in case of emergency. He agreed that he was the best choice for making any snap decisions, should the need arise. He glanced over his shoulder again. Still no red lights.

But what was that? He thought he felt the shuttlecraft shake ever so slightly. And something that sounded like a moan. Wind? In two strides he was at the console, checking instruments.

No wind. Must be his trigger finger wound tight.

3

By the time Landon had shot roping up to the summit of the rock-shaped beast and installed the platform lifter, it was nearly dawn. Satisfied with his rigging, he made the last adjustment to the cables and loaded the bin of components. He would need them to build a remote terminal at the point of origin of the emission, and then he would sync it with the main terminal aboard the *Centaurus*. That link, along with the supraluminal particle sensor, should track the trail of the emission, according to Van Pelt's theoretical work. It had never been done before, but Van Pelt had diagrammed it all out before his untimely end. It should work.

Neither Landon nor Inez could make a move, however, to step onto the platform. Goosebumps tickled him. The hairs on the back of his neck rose, as if something charged the air. He could feel it through the flexifabric of his suit and the metallic web of his lining. Nothing from the thin atmosphere surrounding him could penetrate his protection, he told himself, but he froze in place, anyway.

"Say again, Landon."

"I didn't say anything."

"I thought I heard a voice," Inez said.

"It wasn't me. Must've been Chico from the shuttle." He flicked on the long-range link. "Chico? We've got a bad connection. Please repeat."

Silence answered him.

"Chico?"

Static made him flinch. They'd had to assemble the antenna array too quickly. Had someone made a mistake?

"I'm here," said Chico, panting over the link. "Had to take a piss."

"So you were not trying to reach us a moment ago?" Inez frowned through her faceplate at Landon.

"I'm alone here, remember?" Chico sounded resentful.

"Very well, carry on." Inez nodded at Landon and stepped

onto the platform. "We are going to see one magnificent sunrise, and I do not wish to miss it."

He stepped beside her and set the gears for their ascent. This lifter should work well; assembling it from scavenged parts had been similar in concept to the one he'd constructed for his childhood treehouse in the mountains near Vancouver. Even as a child, he'd been reaching for a closer view of the stars through the instruments he was forever building.

Now, they stared silently at the wall of the mesa as they rose along the beast's flank. Their helmet lights showed nothing but smooth blackness. Occasional lines. Perhaps the lines were cracks. Ruy's scanners had indicated this formation was hollow, so there must be a way inside.

A cramp speared his gut. He took several slow, deep breaths, but the cramp wouldn't go away.

When the lift stopped at the top, traces of the planet's ring defined a dull red arch across a sky that was growing less dark. Inez nudged him and pointed over their shoulders toward the mountains lining the western horizon. Low above them, so low that it was almost setting, was a brilliant star dominating all the stars in the sky.

Landon sucked in his breath. Sol, their own Sun, giver of life, their point of origin. Brandt had told them to expect Sol to appear in the constellation of Cassiopeia, the queen, becoming its sixth, naked-eye star.

At the periphery of his vision, a GPS readout displayed in his helmet, based on the imaging they'd done from orbit and fed into the satellites they'd launched. The glowing green lines shifted as he stepped carefully from the platform, onto the slope of the face, angled like the side of a lumpy mountain. Their boots crunched into a layer of regolith that smoothed out the details of the facial features. Half a kilometer away rose the cone of a hill, which represented the nose. Beyond that, a canyon wall suggested the rise to the forehead. Whatever material composed the shell of this massive structure, regolith covered it everywhere, deposited by millennia of carbon dioxide winds.

"It should not be," Inez whispered. "Ruy says it's sandstone. Why has the wind not eroded it?"

But erosion was the least of Landon's concerns. "Ruy also said it's hollow." He hesitated again, glancing uneasily about him. The tingling sensation that he'd felt earlier had returned, only this time it was much stronger. Here on top, it looked like a lumpy mountainside that stretched away from them, nearly a kilometer in breadth.

Inez held the silent SLP sensor and headed in the general direction of the chin. Landon lifted the bin and followed her. From the examinations of their survey imaging from orbit, he knew the uneven terrain they now moved across represented the hairline meeting the cheek. They were two ants, crawling across the face of a sleeping giant. What would happen, he wondered, if they roused it?

4

Damn them for denying Chico something important to do. Sure, he was on com desk duty, but even a simpleton could track the satellites they'd launched and adjust the antennas that kept their communication network online. What other treatment did he expect? He was mainly their pilot, and he'd already fulfilled the first part of his job by flying the shuttlecraft down here from the orbiting *Centaurus*. It had been no small matter to set it down precisely here, and not there, but had they praised his skill?

Not enough.

For the next ninety days, he would have few responsibilities other than housekeeping chores and com desk duty. At the end of those ninety days, he had to fly them back to the orbiting ship. Inez could probably do it too, but she'd likely screw it up, and they didn't have enough fuel for last-minute adjustments that would become necessary to correct any mistakes. He cracked his knuckles. He didn't like having only enough fuel for one return trip, but that's what the bosses back home had decreed. Foolish bastards. So his job was actually the most important one of all, because he *wouldn't* screw it up. He was the best, hands down. The others depended on him, but did they appreciate him?

Not enough.

He turned back to the east viewport, but he couldn't even pace there properly. This lowered gravity wouldn't let him move in anything less than an undignified bounce.

If Chico had been in charge of the landing party, instead of Inez Pereira, he'd have done things differently. But he hadn't been the best political choice for the job. It was Chico's bad luck that he'd been born in the wrong country, a century too late, an X-chromosome short, the child of a one-night stand. Because of those handicaps, he'd been forced to come to another solar system to seek his fortune. Being male, illegitimate, and Hispanic counted for shit these days.

Don't kid yourself, Chico, he whispered, rolling his eyes heavenward. It was always the same thing for him: getting turned down by authority figures.

The planet's ring glittered in the dusky heavens like a red halo, hailing the forthcoming dawn. It stretched from the eastern horizon, crossed the median, and dove into the mountain range behind base camp where the sandy *mare* ended abruptly. He suspected that even with Alpha and Beta high in the sky, those mountains would remain perpetually cloaked in darkness.

"*Centaurus* to shuttle, come in please."

Chico jumped when the sound of Margot Brandt's voice burst across the com link. He turned from the viewport and hurried back to the console.

"Torres here. Go ahead." It was nice to be able to see another face, even if the solar astronomer's was too wrinkled to suit him. Seeing anybody's face took the edge off his loneliness.

She cleared her throat and began the status update in a rush of words tumbling through her clenched jaw. It was the typical, pained-looking grimace of the hard-assed way she'd been trained. If she wasn't strong enough to take it, then she had no business in space doing a man's job.

"One more thing," she said, when he thought her report was done. "We received an Earthside message for Landon—via radio."

"About time it got here."

She didn't laugh. "Are you ready for relay?"

"Well, I dunno if I can handle that much excitement. Things are kind of busy here."

"Suit yourself."

"Just kidding—"

But she'd cut the voice part of the communication.

"...Sweetheart," he said to emptiness while staring at a

blank screen. Folding his arms across his chest, he fumed at the instruments and waited as the transmission copied. A message for Landon, bah.

The transmitter's quiet humming almost had a hypnotic effect on him. When he heard something like sandpaper sawing against the exterior of the shuttle, he looked up from his instruments with surprise. This time it was the wind. It was definitely picking up outside.

Jesucristo!

And then the coils on one of Ruy's instruments to the right of his elbow started to spring. He couldn't believe his eyes. This planet wasn't as dead as they'd thought. The seismometer was recording nearby activity.

5

The sky lightened rapidly as Landon trekked with Inez. He breathed deeply to control the unsettled pounding of his heart. Conserving energy, neither of them spoke. And even if he didn't need to save his strength, Landon wouldn't have been able to find the appropriate words to describe the awe he felt. Yes, it was awe that guided him under the starlit sky of an extrasolar planet.

And soon, the dawn. Dawn would bring the first of a pair of alien suns over the horizon. He glanced up to find comfort in the familiarity of star patterns. The constellations hadn't changed significantly, aside from that extra star in Cassiopeia. He wasn't so far from home, the stars seemed to be reminding him.

They walked briskly for ten minutes and paused finally to

catch their breaths before the western end of a deep crevasse. A giant slash in the mountainside, it resembled gargantuan lips parted in wonder. A reddish aura permeated the air, enveloping them. The wind suddenly arose and picked up a small dust eddy by his boots and swirled it along in front of him, down into the mouth. A wail pierced through his helmet and tweaked his heartstrings. Unable to resist, he dropped the bin and followed the dust eddy into the mouth.

"Landon!" Inez shouted at him. "What do you think you're doing? We stay together, remember?"

He'd slid to the bottom. The rocky fissure soared above his head, twice his height. What had just happened? He couldn't help thinking of the image of being swallowed into a giant's mouth. But it was merely a canyon, he told himself. A narrow canyon. Not a mouth.

He shivered and looked up at Inez leaning over the edge of the rim above. "I thought I heard something," he explained, feeling the heat of a flush envelop him.

He'd heard the wind. Nothing more.

"Well," Inez answered, sliding down the slope toward him. She dragged his bin with her. "We may as well start looking for the source of the emission here as anywhere. What better place to communicate than through a mouth?"

Reminding himself that he was not afraid, he took his bin of parts from her and pressed on, leading the way across the floor of the mouth canyon. It stretched ahead nearly a third of a kilometer. Regolith crunched beneath his boots here, as everywhere. Dust deposited by the wind over time froze together into granules and piled up in the corners and crevices of sheer walls.

Midway through the mouth, they came to a break in the northern wall. Some geological disturbance had separated the rock, depositing a pile of rubble onto the floor of the mouth.

"Ruy should see this," he said, nodding at the break. Through the opening, he spied a crater several kilometers away on the horizon. His body hair stood up under his liner. He squirmed, but he couldn't shake the unidentified feeling that tickled him.

Then the SLP sensor started to ping. Debris moved at their feet. Springing back, his arm jerked up to shield his head. "Cave-in!" he shouted.

However, nothing fell from above. He scrambled for handholds and footholds to lurch his way up the break in the canyon wall. Unsettled dust, radiating a luminescent glow, rose from the floor of the mouth in pulsating waves. He blinked to clear his vision, but something still glowed, sparkling, bathing the silvery appendages of Inez's suit with a faint touch of violet. She moved slowly, awkwardly, as if in slow motion. Perhaps it was the wispy luminescence that was distorting her movement and his perception. Reaching a hand to her through the funnel of waves, he hoped the corder was sensitive enough to pick up the distorted air. The spot where he had stood only a moment ago was throbbing now, emitting concentric waves of a neon glow of violet dust. It swelled into a mound, and pebbles rolled down its side, scratching and scattering before the disturbance.

A red aura brightened over his shoulder, and he turned in time to see Alpha, looking like a blood-shot eye, lift slowly above the horizon. The star rose, aligned over the distant crater and the fissure where Landon clung. Reddish light seeped through the fissure like a spotlight that aimed into the cloud of violet dust. The colors blended to a purplish red as they met atop the swollen pile of rocky debris.

It continued to swell.

From the middle of the mound, a thumb and knuckle emerged, and then the rest of the *human* hand broke through the alien soil, pressing upward, toward them. Reaching toward the light of an alien dawn.

Chapter Three

The life-sized hand rose through the rubble of clumped soil and rocks. It looked human, but Landon's reasoning denied what his eyes showed him. It couldn't be. Not *here*. Not on this dead, alien world.

And yet... A fist, looking very much alive, looking very *human*, its fingers looking solidly thick like a man's, reached up through the ground only a few meters away from Landon's boots. He felt frozen in time, hearing only the microphone amplification of his own ragged breathing as he watched, distanced by the protective shell of his spacesuit. He blinked, but the fist was still there, snaking farther up into the poisonous, frigid air.

Its thumb slipped between its index and middle fingers. The fist made a *figa* with its hand. Like Inez's necklace.

Did she see it, too? From his peripheral vision, he saw that she stood as frozen as he, here at the bottom of the narrow canyon shaped like a mouth. A human mouth. Spitting out a human hand in the shape of a Brazilian *figa*. On an alien world.

The fist must be attached to a man buried alive.

Landon's knees quivered.

Whatever his eyes were showing him, he at least recognized the geological disturbance that was occurring. He and Inez should be sprinting away from the danger, scaling the canyon wall, using one of the cracks in the sandstone walls to work their way up out of this death trap that would surely collapse on them at any moment.

He swallowed the lump in his throat and looked again. The hand shaped into a *figa* was still there. Rising higher now, as did the sun. Alpha Centauri A. The first sun rose above the horizon and cast a faint light through the break in the canyon wall, spotlighting this erupting hand. It was just enough light to paint the lifeless regolith a deep red.

Except, it wasn't lifeless.

And red was the color of spilled blood.

The fist strained against the barriers of rock and soil. Rocks tumbled away, soil slid aside, but none of those scratching, whooshing noises picked up on Landon's microphones. The absence of sound, other than his own gasping breath and thudding pulse, felt like a heavy shield, locking him in place, flash-freezing him in time, separating him from the action, as if he watched a silent movie. An event that wasn't really happening, not in his reality.

Veins stood out on the back of the alien or maybe human fist, criss-crossing like purple ridges. A sparkly dust cloud hovered above the hand and spun, spinning into the shape of a funnel, as if trying to suck the hand into its violet nucleus.

Violet?

The heavy silence suddenly exploded with rattling, screaming sounds. Inez shouted, "Move, move, move!" The SLP sensor, which she held in her gloved hands, clattered like rolling, tumbling bee-bees in a tin can. She pointed it at the rising fist.

Landon jolted from his stupor. His brain screamed at him to move, to help, to climb, to claw. Do something.

His feet wouldn't move.

The bin, which he'd carried here so carefully, slipped from his shoulder. The lid flipped off, and tools and tachcom parts spilled from the container. It had been crammed so full of the gear he would need for his remote terminal, that there'd been no extra room for medical emergency kits, other than a tube of bandaids.

It was a death sentence to the man down there, struggling to fight his way out of his burial site. The man had been buried alive on a dead world.

Inez leapt closer to the straining forearm as it emerged next. She dropped the SLP sensor beside the shifting mound of soil. Then came the elbow.

And biceps. They broke through as strings of muscles quivering, rippling beneath bronze flesh. A tattoo decorated the arm with a geometric design of triangles within triangles. At any moment, the shoulder and head would surface, and Landon had no way to help, no way to protect the buried man from this hostile environment. Not a man, but rather an alien. Whoever he was, he was presenting himself to a certain death in this thin, unbreathable air.

"Help me!" Inez cried, scraping with her gloves at the soil that buried the alien. "Go get a pressure tent from the rover."

But Landon still couldn't move. Something held him frozen in place, as if an invisible weight pressed down on him. And he, without his strength fully regained.

Scarcely a second passed, but maybe it was eternity—he couldn't tell—before the pleading, straining fingers relaxed, breaking apart from the shape of the *figa*. Those strong fingers withered, the sturdy hand collapsed into a limp ball, and the sinewy arm crumpled to the ground. All of that magnificent flesh dissolved into a pile of dust.

At the same time his paralysis released, and Landon sprang to Inez's side. He fell to his knees, pitching himself toward the mound, as if to save the arm from its destruction. Just as the tips of his gloves reached the pile of dust, a gust of wind snatched it away. The eddy picked up the remnants of the hand and cast them away toward Alpha, and now Beta, rising steadily above the cratered horizon.

"Call Chico," Inez said, pawing the ground next to the rattling SLP sensor. "Get some help."

He flicked on the long-range link, but the walls of the mouth canyon blocked reception. Without waiting to hear the captain's further instructions, he scrambled up the break in the wall, up to the open rim at the top of the crevasse. "Chico," he gasped. Such a small exertion to leave him so breathless, he thought with dismay. "Torres, come in, dammit."

After a brief lapse, a snicker responded. "Landon? Is that you, *cussing*? What's wrong? You felt the quake, is that it?"

His first impulse was to tell him he was wrong. It wasn't a quake but a hand... A hand, erupting from the soil, but... No words came out.

"Landon? What is it, *hombre*?"

"Get the doc," he finally managed to gasp. "There's a man out here. He'll need a doctor. And..." Hell, what else?

Silence answered him.

Across the distance, he could feel Chico's disbelief. "Look, I know it sounds crazy, but there's no time for questions. You've got to send Dr. Montague, quick. Let her fly over here in one of the Thin Air Skimmers. Tell her to bring the medical carrier with a pressure tent. And hurry."

A pause, and then, "Wait, am I reading you? Did you say 'a man'? What man?"

"Down there..." He pointed to the bottom of the mouth canyon as if Chico were here to see. "It was a hand, dammit, a human hand, or at least that's what it *looked* like, and it came up through the soil..." He paused, gasping on the difficult words, turning from the view across the plains to the floor of the canyon where the captain worked feverishly. He had to make Chico understand. "All right, I admit, it sounds crazy. But you've got to believe me. There was this *arm*...and...and... If there's an arm, there must be a body buried down there. We'll have to dig him out. You've got to send help."

Silence. He must think he was lying. Well, Chico could be damned. "Look, you think I don't know? Of course it shouldn't have happened, but I know what I saw! It was a human hand! Inez is down there with him now."

"Uh, where is it now?" Chico asked softly. "This hand?"

Landon sputtered with impatience. "Flesh can't survive long out here, not unprotected in this environment."

"So it blew up?" Chico choked on his words. "On its own? Why don't you bring back some blood and bone fragments for the doc to do a DNA analysis?"

"No, it didn't blow up," Landon shouted. "It blew away. It dissolved into dust and blew away!"

"With triple-point pressure?"

"I know, but—"

"Hold on," Chico said, suddenly sober and crisp. "We're

showing another quake, and this time it looks like a big one."

Almost immediately, Landon noticed that the ground was shaking, slowly at first.

"Inez!" he shouted. "Get out of there!"

But it was too late. A flash of purple erupted above his head and sliced the sky with a streak of color. It looked like an aurora, except that it flickered from the zenith overhead and reached down to touch the wall of the canyon beneath his feet. With one swift stroke of violet light, sandstone trembled. The two sides of the break in the canyon wall ripped farther apart, as if a celestial knife had sliced through the wall. An avalanche of rocks and soil tumbled down, where the stirred-up dust cloud hovered in a pool of deep purplish magenta at the bottom of the canyon. Where the captain knelt. She looked up from her work as pieces of debris rained down on her, and she shielded her head with her arms.

Landon watched helplessly from the top. The ground shifted beneath his feet. Rocks rippled with the passage of some universal rumble. Swaying, he felt as if an invisible punch tried to knock him down.

"Inez!" he shouted, trying to focus on her, but his vision blurred, and he saw two of her outlines.

The cloud swirled around her double image. He blinked again and again, but he could not clear his vision. The dusty whirlpool rose up to meet the purple aurora and caught Inez and her double in its center. Debris tumbled into the funnel of dust as the whirling cloud rose up around Inez's torso. Then her helmet and extended arms.

"Inez!" he shouted again, but she was gone.

The instability ended, as quickly as it had begun. A cloud

of violet had swallowed her. And then dissipated. Pebbles slid down the canyon walls in a final spray. Silence settled in afterwards. Still teetering at the rim, Landon stared at the fresh rubble heaped into the bottom of the canyon. Nothing human showed through the stirred-up dust. Rust colored, not violet at all. Nothing silvery indicated the flexifabric of the captain's suit. Neither bin nor tachcom parts. No insistent pinging of the SLP sensor. There was nothing but rubble.

And silence.

2

¡Carajo!

Chico's fist slammed against the armrest of his pilot's seat as he spoke into the com to Ruy Schulz, that fancy-assed geologist. "You and the doc get back here on the double."

"Now?" Doc said, interrupting like she usually did. "There is much work to do here assembling base, and—"

"Yes, now," Chico snapped. "There's an emergency over at the object. They need a doc."

"Injuries?"

He nodded, even though they couldn't see each other. "Cave-in. Pereira."

"What is her condition?"

"Unknown. I lost the link with Landon."

"All right, on our way. Let's go, Ruy."

After that, Chico heard no more from the construction team, not until they returned a few achingly long minutes later through the shuttlecraft's airlock.

Doc marched immediately to the ladder accessing the

overhead bay that held two of the Thin Air Skimmers, like the one Chico had test-piloted on Mars. Ruy headed straight for the instrument panel at the science station.

"Come on, Ruy," she said, pausing to glance over her shoulder. "We can't waste time getting to the captain."

"A minute..." Ruy said, frowning at the seismogram's readout.

"We may not have a minute," Doc said, her voice shrill. "If her suit has ruptured..."

The two of them stared at each other silently, the uncompleted statement burning the air between them. If the captain's suit had ruptured, then no one could get to her in time.

"I'll come," Chico said.

"You're not suited up." Doc clutched the bars and pulled herself easily up to the catwalk above their heads.

Chico was fast getting into his suit, but it still took time, more time than Ruy's minute. Following her, he clambered up the metal rungs to the skimmer bay. "One more thing you should know," he called after Doc. "Landon says he found something. A man."

That stopped her. "A *man*?" Her voice echoed through her helmet's speaker.

"A man." Chico sprang lithely onto the catwalk behind her. "His story, not mine." He tapped in the sequence to unlock the TASK bay.

"You mean, an alien?" Ruy looked up from his work at the console below and gasped. "And this creature is alive?"

"Look, all I know is what he said." Chico pulled open the door to the first of their pair of skimmers. "The cave-in ended the transmission. But just before it ended, he screamed at the captain. Said she was 'gone.' Someone better get over there pronto."

Doc nodded and stepped inside the lightweight flying machine. "I was afraid something like this might happen."

"You expected Landon to find a man over there?"

"*Non.* He is hallucinating about that, of course."

Chico shook his head. "Landon's not the type."

"It has nothing to do with 'type.' It is the endorphins. Sometimes they are seen following thaw procedure, post-cryogenically. In enough quantities to produce hallucinations."

Unease spread through Chico. "You think that explains what Landon saw?"

"It's possible."

"Did you find any indication of that problem while we were still aboard the *Centaurus*?"

"Test results following his awakening showed suspicious levels," she said. "I will need to consult with one of my colleagues to be sure."

"So you saw these endorphins?"

Her helmet barely nodded. "Let's go, Ruy," she said, turning to the automatic controls.

"Don't mess with that." Chico shoved her fingers away from the control pad. "I'll set the program, and you won't touch it. We only have two of these babies for short flights while we're down here, and we can't afford for you to wreck one of them."

She ignored him, as usual. "Finish up, Ruy."

Chico tapped in the necessary information for the skimmer to fly two novices to the object without a real pilot. "I don't get it. How could there be an endorphin problem? We all passed the screening tests, pre and post."

"We still do not know enough about cryogenics to screen for such a possibility. And besides, there are treatments for hallucinations." She patted her beltpac containing her emergency medical kit. "That part is easy."

"I don't believe it. Not Landon."

"It has nothing to do with the level of testosterone." She raised her voice to a nasal pitch, sharp enough that it induced chills. "Let's go *now*, Ruy. We need an expert digger over there."

"I've got the epicenter," Ruy said, pointing at the screen before him. "It seems to be in the sphinx's mouth." He stood up, shook his head, and hurried to the ladder leading to the catwalk.

3

Landon was still scrabbling with his gloves, pushing away rocks and dirt, frantically scraping through the debris, searching for Inez—all to no avail—when the humming sound of one of their skimmers buzzed overhead. About time help arrived.

He was still on his hands and knees, scratching at the alien soil, when a gentle bump from behind made him look up. Ruy stood there, offering him one of his pro-diggers. It was basically a smart shovel, motorized and equipped with sensors and pre-set programs. This should find Inez, if anything would.

But even after Alpha and Beta completed a quarter of their daily journey across the sky, there was still no sign of her. Landon worked side-by-side with Ruy and Doc, digging into the base of the sphinx's mouth. Their probings pockmarked the landfill of the cave-in and turned up nothing. Inez just wasn't here. Nor anyone else. No armless alien. None of his tachcom parts.

Landon paused his digger and glanced up at the dusky, lavender sky, bisected by a filmy ring. At mid morning, the distant pair of stars glowed like dying embers through the dust content their digging disturbance had cast into the atmosphere. Shadows filled the inside of the mouth, making it harder to see the sensors that would indicate a nearby, anomalous object.

He had clearly seen the tattooed arm rising through the regolith. And what about the captain? Hairs prickled the back of his neck.

They should've found her by now. They should all be back in the shuttlecraft, or maybe their brand-new base, exploring the questions that had been raised, moving on to other problems. The captain, an armless body, Landon's bin of tachcom parts, and a pinging supraluminal particle sensor should all be here, but they weren't. The giant mouth-like formation of rock had opened up and swallowed them.

He turned back to his digging with renewed effort. Over the whir of its motor, he heard disjointed phrases. He couldn't distinguish Ruy's voice from the doc's, but he realized it didn't matter, as they registered the same complaint.

"Useless...it's been too long."

"Life support...too low."

"Cannot endanger the rest of the mission..."

Finally, Landon felt someone tugging on his arm. He turned off the digger and looked up. "Montague" was written across the helmet of the spacesuited figure pulling at him.

"Landon, you must stop now, yes?" Doc said, lowering her voice to a nasal softness he'd never thought possible from her.

"We only need a little more time. We can still save her."

"It's not your fault."

He shook her off. "She could still be alive, trapped under the rubble. Maybe her oxygen tank withstood the accident. But if we don't get to her in time, then she *will* suffocate in..." He glanced at the stats in his peripheral vision indicating the remaining supply in his own suit. "...About an hour." He reached for the digger to resume his work.

"Landon," Doc said softly, "we've done enough. It's time to quit. Even if we find the captain now, she's not likely to be alive. We must not endanger our own air supplies. We need some time to reach the rover, yes? Twenty minutes? We have to go there because the skimmer we flew over here has no suit renewer. We will have to come back for it later."

"She's right, Landon," Ruy said in his slow, maddeningly calm voice. "If Captain Pereira were down there, the sensors would've detected her by now."

"Half an hour more," Landon said. "That's all I ask."

4

Chico tightened the last connection that would bring their habitat to life and cheered softly. It had taken him half the time that it would've taken the scientists to finish assembling the bubbles of their base. As soon as Doc and Ruy had flown away in the skimmer, Chico had suited up and crossed the rocky terrain on foot. It wasn't so far from the shuttlecraft to their new base. Those scientists thought they were smart, but they'd left a half-assed job of erecting the shell. He took it from there, pressurizing the two bubbles and bringing power to the equipment. Finally, he removed his spacesuit, breathed in the new, plastic-smelling air, and didn't die. He plugged his suit into the renewer closet and got to work connecting the command station.

Now that it was all hooked up, the com link's display flashed to life. The *Centaurus's* orbit would pass overhead in a few more minutes.

He cracked his knuckles and stretched, lifting himself up onto tiptoes, reaching high above his head. The domed ceiling of this bubble yawned beyond his outstretched fingers. He pumped his arms like windmills and failed to strike anything.

Maybe it was too large in here. Or maybe he just didn't like being alone.

A blinking dot appeared in the upper left corner of the tracking screen to indicate the orbiter's path overhead. Simultaneously, the com link started to crackle.

"*Centaurus* to shuttlecraft, come in please," said Margot Brandt. Her precise tone sounded strained.

"Torres here. And I'm reporting from our newly operational base, not the shuttlecraft. Go ahead—" *Sweetheart*, he started to say, but he bit his tongue in time.

"You guys sustain any damage from that energy burst?"

He frowned. "Negative." He saw no point in alarming them unnecessarily about Pereira, considering Landon's apparent endorphin attack.

Brandt's breathless voice raced on. "...our orbit is deteriorating. At this current rate, we'll intersect the plane of the planet's ring, possibly as soon as thirty-three hours."

Chico stiffened. "Say again, *Centaurus*?"

Patiently, Brandt restated the situation. Then her voice lost its confidence. "I don't get it. The readout on the fuel reserves must be wrong. It shows we're too low, but we didn't use *that* much for our mid-flight corrections on our way out here. You know anything about a leak?"

Chico felt a rumbling in the pit of his stomach.

"Orbital corrections *here*," she continued, "will leave our fuel supplies too low for mid-flight maneuvers on our way home. It's too close, and the commander doesn't like it. She's considering an abort in another thirty hours."

Abort? He felt a wave of panic, then suppressed it. "Everyone's over at the object, and I can't raise them. Too much atmospheric interference."

Static responded, and he wondered if she'd heard him. Finally, she said, "Another alternative is to find ourselves some more fuel."

Chico leaned forward and spoke crisply into the com. "Roger, I copy." More fuel!

Brandt continued. "Fortunately, we have a major source of fuel nearby in Proxima Centauri, and we have an expert aboard ship at helium-3 separation. Commander Masambwa, who cut her teeth on the Jupiter Project, remember?"

He swallowed hard. *Jesucristo.*

"Remember?"

"Yeah." Who could forget? That's why they'd chosen her to be commander and not someone else, someone more capable, someone less prone to risk.

"Anyway," Brandt went on, "she says we'll be gone about a week. Think you could get by without us that long?"

Sure, the *Centaurus* had shields to protect them from solar radiation, but he estimated there was only a 50-50 chance they were strong enough to withstand a dip into a star. Even a dim one like Proxima Centauri. What was Masambwa thinking? Had she lost her mind to even consider such an alternative?

The ship would most likely burn up. Then how would Chico get home? But what he said in his pilot's voice instead was, "No problem."

Long after his conversation with Brandt ended, he tried the link once again to surface communications and crossed his fingers. "Come in, Doc. TASK I, do you read me?"

Nothing. Wearily, he pulled off the headset and laid it down. Moving through the two bubbles of base, he adjusted all the connections that would flood this alien place with light.

5

The muscles in Landon's back burned as he bent over his digger, guiding it into the rubble of the cave-in. He didn't care about his own aches. Soreness meant he was alive. He didn't know if he could say the same for Inez.

His breath caught in his throat, tasting of plastic. Feeling light-headed, he swayed on his feet. Must be running low on oxygen. And still, without any signs of the captain.

Perhaps twenty minutes had passed when Doc joined him. She'd been up on the rim of the mouth, and now she slid down the slope into the bottom of the canyon. "I finally reached Chico," she said with a gasp.

Ruy powered down his digger, and Landon looked up from his work. His fingers tensed on the handle, idling his tool rather than shutting it off.

Doc raced on with her words, stumbling over them. "I could barely hear him. He said something about 'trouble' with the Centaurus. They want us to return immediately. The base is fully inflated now. Chico finished assembling it. Let's go."

67

Landon's heart froze. Molly was aboard the *Centaurus*. "What sort of trouble?"

"I don't know." She turned and reached for the first ledge that stair-stepped out of the canyon.

His digger, still whining softly, slipped from his hands as Landon surveyed his work. It seemed such a waste. In only a few more minutes he might've found Inez. She was buried here, somewhere, along with the rest of his equipment and the remains of that tattooed, alien arm—the Tititri.

Ruy scrambled out of his hole, stumbling over his feet in his haste. Unsettled dust swirled around him as he shoved his digger into the tool carrier.

Doc paused on one of the ledges of the slope for an instant, then said, "Looks like the wind's picking up. We'd better hurry. Landon, you are coming, yes?"

"On my way."

Ruy shouldered his bin of tools and crawled up the break in the canyon's wall toward Doc. Dust and sand, carried by the wind, coiled around them.

Doc's voice pierced Landon's helmet. "Now, Dr. Walker."

She turned and climbed up out of sight into a film of gathering dust.

Pebbles dislodged from the side of the canyon as Ruy readjusted his load. "Hurry, Landon. Dust storm coming up fast." He sprang up to the next ledge, following Doc.

"I'm right behind you."

Except, he wasn't.

A dust eddy rose from the canyon floor, obscuring his view of the rim where the doc and Ruy were headed. Not seeing them, he felt more alone than ever. Something about being alone on an alien world sent a charge of panic shooting through him like an electric bolt.

"Hey, guys," Landon said through his transmitter. He tensed his muscles to follow them.

Except, his feet wouldn't move.

Static answered him instead of their voices. His nerves prickled. Something glued him here to the bottom of the mouth canyon. He glanced down at the evidence of their morning's labor. Empty holes.

Pebbles slid against his boots, where he stood, frozen. Dirt whirled across the ground and sprayed into his excavations.

He looked again. It wasn't so empty down there. Something glimmered.

At his feet, the dust churned more rapidly, redefining itself into the shape of a funnel. He tried to move, but he couldn't make his arms and legs work. Something tugged at him, something that felt like the pressure of added weight. His head felt so heavy that he thought it would sink him down to the sparkles glowing through the regolith.

A glowing cloud like this one had taken Inez.

It must've been his martial arts training that gave him the necessary surge of adrenaline to break free. Scrabbling away from his diggings, he felt himself grow lighter with each centimeter of distance gained from whatever was pulling at him from the bottom of the hole. Leaving his digger behind, he crawled up to the first ledge, gasping. Rocks and chunks of debris spun round and round along the floor of the mouth canyon. He'd stood there just a couple of heartbeats ago. Down there, the ground split farther apart. The hole he'd dug widened into a bowl, and a thick cloud of dust mushroomed out.

Beneath the dust, something that looked like a tunnel resolved from the murk. A tunnel of violet light rose up from inside the sphinx, illuminating rough walls. It was an entrance. Into the sphinx.

This doorway would give him a chance to find Inez. Maybe even the Tititri. But the readout of his suit's stats in his peripheral vision flashed a yellow warning. He didn't have much time left of his air supply. If he went down there now, he was a dead man.

Chapter Four

Landon crouched, hesitating on the first ledge above the floor of the mouth canyon. A steady flash of yellow light pulsed across his line of vision inside his helmet and finally pulled his attention away from the glittering violet tunnel entrance into the sphinx. He would be dead without oxygen. The yellow light reminded him to choose life.

"I'm sorry," he whispered, knowing Inez couldn't hear him, even if she was at the bottom of that tunnel. He rose, stretching his stiff knees, and slowly inched up the break in the wall of the canyon. Ledges protruded from a ramp of rubble that led to the rim above.

He wasn't giving up, he told himself. For now, he had to retreat to the rover to plug his suit into the renewer. After that, he'd return with more oxygen for Inez. He'd left his tools down there, and with them he would enter the tunnel that had swallowed her. He wouldn't give up until he'd found her, along with the rest of his tachcom gear, which the instability had taken. Maybe he'd find the armless alien, too. And the Tititri.

He couldn't afford to delay long, for Inez's sake. With Ruy's and the doc's help, they'd make it back in time. But when he finally hauled himself up over the rim of lips defining the mouth canyon, he saw nothing. No one.

Up here, atop the face of the sphinx, a gale had lifted sand into the air. Sand sprayed against him, rattling against the flexifabric of his suit, trying to push him off his feet. No wonder his companions had been in such a hurry to leave. Panic seized him as he struggled to maintain his balance. Down below in the mouth, the canyon walls had protected him and his colleagues from the brunt of these winds, but up here, on top of the mesa, where the sphinx tilted its head up toward space, the wind blew unobstructed. Sand, along with dust, obliterated visibility and scratched against his suit.

"Ruy!" he shouted. "Doc!"

They didn't answer.

He toggled the GPS, but no map came up inside his helmet. Nothing except the flashing yellow light. Combined with its glare and the shifting dust, he couldn't see much beyond a meter or two. A form moved ahead, just at the edge of visibility. It had to be one of them.

"Wait for me," he called. His voice echoed against the inner shell of his helmet, bouncing off the pulsating yellow light of warning.

They still didn't answer.

His pulse quickening, he lurched forward and stumbled over an oblong object lying loose on the ground. It looked like one of Ruy's tools. Ruy must have dropped it.

Landon leaned over to scoop it up. At first, it surprised him that the small piece of equipment was heavier than its size indicated. He had to readjust his grip and balance, lifting the weight.

It wasn't a tool.

From its shape, it looked like a femur. But it felt heavy and solid, like a rock. Not a bone.

Clutching the object, he staggered on his feet, fighting to regain his balance. He lowered his chin and head butted into the wind, fighting his way through the mixture of sand and dust.

Something told him that what he carried was in fact a bone. Not brittle and dried out, but preserved somehow... Maybe it had come from the body that went with that hand. It was impossible to make any sense of it. Seeing that tunnel disappearing down into this face structure gave him hope that perhaps Captain Pereira...Inez...wasn't dead.

She *would* be dead when her air ran out.

As would he, the yellow light seemed to be saying.

He struggled along, encumbered by the heaviness of the bone. The wind tugged at its length, trying to wrest it from his grip.

An alien bone! He couldn't wait to hand it over to Doc for analysis.

He tightened his hold on the femur, if that's what it was, and moved forward, blind to his direction. Damn the GPS for not working. Satellite must be down. He had to judge his way from the upward slope of the smooth terrain beneath his boots. This slope, he reasoned, would be the hump that shaped the cheek.

The cheek beneath him rumbled suddenly, and its vibration traveled up through his legs. Pausing to balance himself against the movement, he gripped the bone tighter against his chest. Inside his helmet, the yellow light flashed orange in his peripheral vision.

His pulse throbbed against his temple. He couldn't think clearly. Had he lost track of that much time?

"Ruy," he gasped.

But all that answered on any of the channels of his link was static.

The aftershock died, but his knees continued to tremble. He staggered on, and before long he stumbled into a depression, which he thought represented the hairline. That meant he was more than halfway to the mesa's edge, the terminus of the lift. He'd constructed the device only a few hours ago to bring them up here from the plains two hundred meters below.

He stepped more cautiously across the ridges. The edge couldn't be far away. One wrong step could tumble him over the edge. Even in one-third gravity, the slow fall would kill him.

He peered ahead into the sand but could not see the lift.

It had to be here.

"Doc?" He called into the sand, but there was no answer.

He'd used up his luck long ago, and now he was alone, always alone, stumbling along the length of this alien formation...

"Lannndonnnn..." He thought he heard voices.

No, it wasn't voices of his colleagues but the wind, moaning around him, through him. It must be a case of audio matrixing, his brain trying to make sense out of sounds.

More important, where was the lift? Had Ruy and the doc found it, or were they as lost as he was?

He wasn't lost. He knew exactly where he was. Somewhere along the western perimeter of the sphinx's mesa top. The lift was only a few more meters away. But he couldn't see it from here.

Acid burned in his stomach, and the orange light continued to blink at him. Soon, it would turn to red, and then he'd suffocate.

He turned right and had to adjust to the sideways buffeting

of the wind. The alien bone that he carried, the proof that he was not mad, slipped again, weighing him down, and he readjusted his grip.

Suddenly, he tripped over a cable stretched knee-high in front of him. Through the gloom of dust, he saw the grapnel, caught in the rocky ridges of this alien sphinx's hair. It was holding the skeletal structure containing the pulley. He followed the cable to the mesa's edge, but there was no platform. It had to be at the bottom, then, and it must've recently lowered Ruy and Doc to the plains below.

Without him.

2

Chico paced as much as the lowered gravity would allow him the dignity of pacing through the empty, sciencey sterile modules of base. Too damned empty. There were no frayed pictures from home tacked up to cabinet doors yet. From the pop-top console of his command station, where he was left behind and "in charge" as Pereira's puppet, it was eight gliding strides over to the wall of his cage. Yeah, that's what this place really was, a *cage*. Dressed out only to look like their base. Home away from home, here on the surface of this planet.

His momentum rebounded him against the slack curve of the wall, giving him a nose full of plastic reek. *Snort.* This cage was an under-inflated bounce house, that's what. A loose sheet crinkled and flapped where there should be a connector into the habitation module. His mates had done a sloppy job erecting these two bubbles, but what else could he expect from them? They were only scientists. They weren't as qualified as he, a military man with bastard pedigree. But those scientists. Hell, they couldn't even handle the simple task of assembling their base, and yet the captain, who also wasn't as qualified as Chico, had chosen them, the scientists, and not him, for all the important jobs.

He punched aside the loose sheet of plastic—at least the two modules sealed properly together, otherwise he'd be dead—and ducked into the habitation module, where crates still littered the floor space. He knew which one to open. He pulled out the empty shells of dumbbells and carried them back with him into the work module, eight more gliding steps back to the bucket of sand, waiting to be examined in the lab.

He filled the dumbbells with local sand, pushed a crate over to his console, and used it as a bench to methodically lift, lower and alternate weights while watching for updates to come through the command console.

Something was wrong. They should've abandoned the site and returned to the rover by now. Their suits should be plugged into the renewer, their feet should be up, and they should be sipping piña coladas. But whatever was happening over there, where history was being made without him, there wasn't a damned thing Chico could do about it.

He grunted with each exhalation and tried to ignore his impotence. He laid down the weights and moved closer to the console. "Base to rover, come in please."

Nothing. He adjusted the controls, which shifted the angle of the antenna aimed in their direction.

"Landon, do you read me? Schulz? Doc?"

But all that answered him was the scratchy gargle of atmospheric interference.

"Base to *Centaurus*."

Again, nothing. He slammed down his headset and went back to his weights.

Wind gnawed at the outer fabric of the bubbles, and he paused his lifting to glance up at the wrinkles of the curved, silver ceiling. A shiver tickled the back of his neck. Then the wind died as suddenly as it had come up, and he let out his breath and began the reps again.

It was in his blood to distrust the wind. His mother had actually feared it, and he was convinced that was the real reason why she'd left the wind farm in Colorado to take the hydroponics job at Eagle City. It was his uncle, the senator Juan "Jota" Torres, who had cashed in a favor and secured the job for Mama in the first place. Too bad the senator had never accepted Chico. If he had, it would've been easier to get into the Academy.

Bah! It was good to be away from them all.

Hsssss. Chico dropped the weights and came to attention. That last noise sounded like leaking air, not the wind. Were the bubbles losing pressure? In one leap he was at the console, checking gauges, but everything appeared normal.

"Landon, would you fucking answer me?"

It was only four strides to the centrally located suit closet, and he glided there to fling open the door. A solitary suit hung there from its stand, "Torres" printed clearly on the helmet. He slammed the door shut, then lurched to the closest viewport and peered outside at the dim day. Lacing his fingers together, he cracked his knuckles, but it didn't make him feel any better.

Disgusted, he turned away and stalked back to the com desk like a caged animal.

Something flapped outside against the Mylar housing, and

then it was gone.

He paused to glance over his shoulder at the viewport. *Had this planet supported life at one time? If so, it was certainly dead now. Rather than being stillborn, like the Moon, planets could actually die.* Instinctively, he crossed himself.

But... If he returned from this mission, bearing enough data to keep a room full of computers busy for a lifetime, he could become even more of a stud. He wouldn't need to rely on good looks to impress the women. He'd be a hero.

He let out his breath and sat down at the com desk. He wondered if the *Centaurus* had left already. That's why they were silent. He was sure.

No. They wouldn't have left without telling him.

With the same respectful fear of a rattlesnake's bite, Chico feared that if the ship left orbit to scoop fuel out of the sun, they wouldn't be coming back.

3

Landon's knees weakened for just a moment, and in that instant, the wind pushed him sideways, out of reach of the pulley. The alien bone that Landon had been gripping tightly dropped to the ground. He made a move to retrieve it, but the wind prevented him from bending over. The orange light throbbed at him, and his breath came in shallow gasps, as if already he had no oxygen.

Ruy and Doc had left without him.

Sand slid scratching against his suit. Summoning strength to his arm, he punched against the wind and grasped the lever that would bring the platform up to him. With a snap of his wrist, he felt the vibration of gears turning. The cable began to move. Slowly.

The hammering of his heart settled a beat or two, and he turned back for the femur, his prize. The wind bullied him a step beyond its reach, and when he bent down, the wind held him there.

Trapped.

His fingers tightened around the bone. How could it be so heavy? He sat there, listening to the cable clank. Suddenly it stopped, and he crawled forward. He peered over the rim of the mesa, but all he saw was a cloud of dusty sand. There was only emptiness where the platform should be.

He pulled himself up along the cable and found the lever again. He jiggled it harder. Nothing happened.

"Doc! Ruy! Help me!"

Eyes closing, tears squeezing from their corners, he focused on his martial arts power. Taking a deep breath, he tried again, slamming his weight into the lever. This time, the cable jerked and groaned and moved.

He panted and clung to the lever and felt the vibration of the sliding cable throb through his body.

Finally, the cable stopped again, but this time the platform had risen from the depths of the sandy swamp below. He fastened the lock and inched his way along, groping around for the bone. He rolled it onto the platform, then crawled after it. He struggled against the wind's fury to release the lock. Clinging to the railing, he felt himself float downward, bumping rhythmically against the side of the cliff.

It seemed an eternity before the platform jolted to a stop, and he realized he'd made it down to the plains. Somewhere nearby should be the rover. He gasped on a shallow breath and blinked at the blinking orange light in his helmet. He tipped his head back to peer up at the silent mountain. It had bested him, but only for now.

He stumbled off the platform, sinking down into soft sand. Ahead in the murk, something scratched with a metallic ring to it. It had to be sand, slamming against the rover's alloy hull.

Then his receiver crackled to life. A shrill sob pierced his ears. "*Mon Dieu!* Finally, you come!"

Doc must've spied him from inside the rover. He'd never before been so glad to hear her.

4

Madre, Chico thought. The Mylar bubbles of base crackled and groaned under the persistent fury of the wind. Then something snapped and scraped against the exterior. The digits of the wind speed monitor died.

He stalked with bouncing leaps from the com desk to the viewport. Nothing to see out there. He swiped at the loose strands of hair that kept sliding into his eyes. Rolled his fingers into a fist. If the winds were so strong, then what if they carried away the shuttlecraft? There'd be no way off this rock, no way back to the *Centaurus.* No way home.

He tried to stomp back to the com desk, but he couldn't even get that much satisfaction. Lowered gravity had fairyfied his legs. The timescreen showed approximately one hour of life left for the field crew. They'd never make it.

He held open the channel and shouted. "Give up on Pereira! Get your butts back here to base. We've got to save ourselves."

Static was the only response.

He couldn't stand around and do nothing for another minute, let alone twenty-four of them, when the *Centaurus* would clear the pole and Masambwa would regain communications, only to tell him again to stay put. What did she want? Their sacrifice?

And what if the aliens showed up? He'd left all their weapons on the shuttlecraft.

Making up his mind, he took the four leaping strides to the suit closet and slipped into his suit in record time. Masambwa would have his balls, he thought, grinning like an idiot boy, about to solo for the first time. He shouldn't have wasted this much time. It was too late for the others, not for him. There was still enough time to save his own neck before the winds ripped apart the entire base camp. He fastened his seals and stepped lightly into the airlock.

When it released him to the outside, he suddenly felt paralyzed. He had struggled in winds before, plenty of times, visiting Mama's family back in Colorado, but nothing like this where he weighed only a third of his mere sixty-three kilos. This must be how a trout felt, fighting the current to move upstream. But the trout could do it, and so could he. He may be the smallest of the crew, but he was the toughest.

It was a good thing he knew where the shuttlecraft sat, because he couldn't see a damned thing. He wished he knew the stride count, the way he'd known inside the modules. Lowering his chin, he stepped out into the wind.

Visibility was about a meter, enough to see where he stepped, one foot at a time. It was not enough, however, to spot the semi-circle of rock soldiers, which stood guard between the twin bubbles of base and the shuttle. He'd put the craft down as close as he'd dared to that arrangement of rocks. He wondered if the wind was strong enough to propel two-meter-high boulders, turning them into giant torpedoes... No, he wouldn't think about that.

When the spindle of one of the giant rocks appeared to his left, rising through the wind-stirred dust and sand, he knew he wasn't very far from the shuttle. Battling the wind made breathing harder, and he paused to rest, fighting to remain upright, standing more or less still. He looked up and saw pieces of a dim sky through wisps of dust. A big dust storm would spread this ground-level murk into the upper atmosphere and make it impossible to return to the *Centaurus*. It was now or never.

A shape loomed ahead in the gloom. It looked like a giant insect, but he knew it was the craft that had carried them here to the surface. *Escape.* He struggled toward it, but a burst of wind pushed him backwards. Sand hissed against his suit and masked the shuttle from sight. Feeling disoriented, he brushed the grit from his faceplate, but it didn't improve his filmy vision.

Something sounded in the surrounding turbulence, like a long, drawn-out groan. An image of his crewmates, bent over their consoles, flashed through Chico's mind. Wasted talent. He blinked, and they were gone. Gone forever from Chico's mind as they would be lost forever on this planet once Chico fired the engines. He shook himself and thought, *it's only the wind.*

Jesucristo, was that a rhythm he heard? It sounded like a prolonged twang, a mechanical sigh, the lament from an electronic cello. The rocks were catching the wind in their cracks and crevices, the same way the *Centaurus's* scoop caught tachyons in its grooves. He sucked in air, and the raspy sound broke the spell.

His conscience was speaking to him through the future ghosts of his crewmates, who were about to be left behind on this planet.

He could picture himself a tumbleweed if he didn't snap out of this. Gritting his teeth, pushing the song from his mind, casting away the specters of the crew, he struggled on toward the spidery outline of the craft ahead in the murk.

5

Landon shook as he ran, staggering to the rover.

He was still shaking some minutes later when he finally stumbled out of the airlock and into the cab of the rover. He dropped the bone carefully into a sample bucket and pulled off his helmet. Breathing deeply, he sucked in the air, spiked with sweating bodies and a metallic tanginess. It seemed a lifetime ago—not mere hours—when they'd driven the rover here. Now, a cocktail of anger that his crewmates had left him and relief that he'd made it and guilt that he survived swept over him.

Doc stood before him, trembling on her feet as she clutched two oxygen tanks, one in each arm. They slipped from her grip and clanged to the aisle floor. "I was on my way back to find you. We had to hurry... If our air had run out, then we would've all been gone." She collapsed against him in an embrace, awkward with the bulk of their suits between them.

He held her for several heartbeats and then guided her gently to the bench seat behind the driver's seat. Ruy sat at the controls.

"I can't believe she's gone," Ruy said, his voice quivering as he started the engine.

"Shut it down." Landon snatched up the fallen canisters of oxygen, rattling them against each other. "We're going back up there."

"Landon," Doc said, her voice quavering at first and then regaining strength, "we're done for now." She pulled on his sleeve as he worked to hook up one canister to his suit. "Tell me what happened out there before Ruy and I arrived."

"I've already told you," he said, shrugging away from her hand.

The rover suddenly lurched forward as Ruy pushed the control stick into gear. Landon staggered in the aisle, bumping against the back of the seat. "Hey! Didn't you hear me? We can't leave yet."

Ruy ignored him and guided the stick slowly, cautiously. "We may not have enough stored power to make it all the way back to base."

"Stop!" Landon shouted, reaching past Ruy for the controls. "We can't leave her up there."

"Landon," Doc said again in that soft voice indicating she knew something he didn't, or perhaps couldn't, understand.

"We have to go back," Landon said, reaching across Ruy to cut the power. "*Now!* Before it's too late."

Doc pulled him away, turning him to face her. "A simple task to go back up there in these winds, *non*? They're strong enough that they already took the skimmer that Ruy and I used for flying over here."

"We don't have any choice," he said, gritting his teeth.

She gave his arm a shake. "We spent the last five hours

looking for her without finding any trace. We don't even have a signal from her suit beacon to guide us in where to look. How do you propose to find her in spite of all that?"

"After the two of you left the site, the bottom fell out of the hole we were digging. It opened up a tunnel. That's where she must be. They took her inside. Don't you see?"

Doc shrank away from him. "They?" She threw a cautious glance at Ruy.

"The Tititri," Landon said. "That tunnel is a way inside this...hell, I don't know what to call it. A hollow mesa?"

"An alien-made sphinx," Ruy said softly.

Landon burned with impatience. They were so close. "Whatever it is," he continued, "whatever is left of the Tititri, they're inside it. And so is Inez. That tunnel is a way to her. And to them. They're the reason we're here. We can't leave now." He thought of the hand emerging before the cave-in and hesitated before adding, "We have to access that tunnel. What else can we do?"

"Hmmm."

Landon had never seen Doc at a loss for words. She opened her mouth, as if to speak, then shut it again. Her focus darted to the seat where her beltpac lay.

Realization dawned on him like a cold, heavy wave of the north Pacific. It crashed through his mind the way breakers used to thunder against the rocky shores of British Columbia where he'd brooded many hours following the Dome bombing that had killed his father. "You don't believe me," he said slowly, drawing out each syllable. "You don't believe I saw what I saw."

Doc chose her next words carefully and shifted her weight again, as if easing away from Landon's rage. "It isn't exactly a question of not *believing* you."

"Then what *exactly* is it?"

"Landon, I know you believe what you saw was real. What's at issue is not the reliability of your report but rather the reliability of the event observed."

"Oh, I see. You think I imagined it. Well, I brought you proof." He pointed to the bucket that held the alien bone.

Her gaze flickered over there. "What, a rock?"

"You'll see what it is when you examine it. But first, we have to go back for Inez."

"As your doctor, I outrank you in such matters regarding the well-being of the mission as a whole, and I'm telling you we cannot afford to continue the search at this time."

His voice rose, shaking. "Is that why you left me behind? For the sake of the mission? What do you think I am—damaged goods?"

She sighed. "You *said* you were right behind us. And then our communication system failed. We assumed you were with us all that time."

"Right. That doesn't explain why you took the platform lifter down without waiting for me."

Her voice quavered. "We were coming back for you."

"With more oxygen from here," Ruy added.

Landon grunted. Maybe. "But what about the captain? Where in *hell* is she? You tell *me*, dammit! Where?"

"There was a tragic accident. As for the rest of your story—"

"Oh, it's a story, is it? How do you think I could ever concoct a story like that? About a hand, from an arm that should be alien but looks human? Huh? How?"

She frowned, and her eyes darted back and forth like a

nervous bird's. "What you are experiencing is post-cryogenic trauma. I can treat it."

"You ought to be treating Inez, not me." Landon's voice dropped to a whisper as the fight evaporated from him. His outburst hadn't helped his case. He'd always been expert at keeping his emotions under control. He hadn't convinced them of the reality of what he'd seen.

"Captain Pereira is beyond our help."

"We can't leave her," he repeated. They glared at each other in impasse.

"Consider this." Ruy twisted around in the driver's seat to face the other two, but he had a way of not looking directly at either of them. "Assuming the captain is still alive, assuming she somehow survived the initial cave-in, and assuming her air canister somehow remained intact, then what's left of her air supply is gone by now. If she's lucky, perhaps there is a trickle left. Even so, we cannot possibly get back up there, not in these winds, and find her in time, before that last dribble of her air runs out."

Landon slammed his fist into the side of the nearest bench seat, causing Doc's beltpac to bounce. Something had gone wrong with his mind while he'd been frozen, and now he couldn't trust anything anymore, not even his own perception.

Abruptly, a stronger gust of wind rocked the rover.

Chapter Five

Chico climbed up the ladder into the shuttle's airlock and cycled through. He entered the tube of the cabin, unfastened his helmet and gloves, and inhaled deeply its welcoming, ozone smells.

A few minutes later he slumped into his pilot's chair wondering if he was mad, if his endorphins had gone hyperactive, too. The wind had captivated him with its song, and he'd allowed it. Maybe all of them were a bunch of crazies for being caught here in this impossible situation.

He could still save himself.

He stared, uncomprehending, at the touchpads and lights and blank screens before him. The faint hum emanating from the computers sounded sterile after the music he'd experienced.

Then Masambwa's monotonal voice startled him, demanding a report. The *Centaurus* hadn't left orbit, as he'd suspected. It had only been out of range, on the opposite side of the planet. Something was screwing with his mind, if he hadn't realized that before.

"The periphery of a major dust storm is upon you, Torres," she said. "From our analysis up here, it appears that it will get much worse before it gets better. We can't leave you down there in it. Take the samples you've already collected and lift off for rendezvous. You can't waste any time, because in approximately two hours we depart to harvest helium from Proxima."

Did the commander never experience emotion, Chico wondered. "Ma'am, the others haven't returned yet—"

"Are you questioning my authority, Lieutenant?"

"No, ma'am." What was wrong with him? Masambwa was giving him permission to do exactly what he'd planned to do: lift off now. Alone. "It's just that all four of them are out there, and one of them needs assistance."

"Negative, Lieutenant. They are scientists. They will understand that in the name of science, the entire mission must not be jeopardized on their account."

"Excuse me, ma'am, but one of them is Captain Pereira." Pereira was military, one of the elite, one of *them*. The military couldn't be compromised.

Masambwa paused slightly before beginning again. "I remind you, Lieutenant, of article IIIf stroke 2d of our code which states that personal sacrifice in the eventuality of emergency situations, such as this one, Lieutenant, are required for the fulfillment of the mission purpose. Captain Pereira was one of the best, and she was well prepared..."

Chico didn't hear the rest. Pereira wasn't a "was," at least not yet. He opened an access panel and poked around inside with the clippers. "What's that, ma'am? I'm not receiving you. Must be a problem here, somewhere. Stand by, and I'll find it." He found the right wire and snipped.

Madre! What had he done? The clippers slipped from his hand as he stared at the jagged ends of wires. *You just threw away your ticket home!*

Some new voice in his mind, higher than Masambwa's authority, nagged at him like the wind music of the rocks, reminding him who he really was beneath the stud exterior—

Mama and the *abuela* had beat it into him enough times down home. He didn't know if he was hearing their ghosts or not, but he understood their message loud and clear. He couldn't abandon the other four. If he had to return to the *Centaurus* without them, it wasn't worth returning at all. What kind of hero would he be if he let them die?

That meant he had to rescue them.

With new resolve, he sprang away from the open panel, retrieved his helmet and gloves, and headed for the ladder to the bay where the last remaining TASK skimmer housed. Flying it alone in those winds outside would be tricky, but nothing was impossible for Chico Torres.

2

An explosion of sand particles rattled against the rover's alloy side like a maraca gone wild. Landon gripped the handlebar and wedged against the bench seat. The vibration of the rover's engine tickled his thighs, indicating that the vehicle moved on its own power. He stared glumly at the backs of Ruy and Doc, who sat in the driver's and navigator's seats, respectively. Beyond them, the console glowed green and the window showed their headlights disappearing into a cloud of dust, stirred up by raging sand. Visibility out there was at an arm's length.

An arm.

Landon shuddered and tried not to think about that alien arm. Nor Inez. This mission was no longer just about Molly, his baby girl. Now he also had to make some sort of sense out of the senselessness of the captain's death. She couldn't have died for nothing. He swore he would find meaning.

Somewhere at the depth of his thoughts, the wind suddenly strengthened to a new level of intensity. A renewed barrage of sand scratched against the windows of the rover. Light winked out and the sound of the engine died. The vehicle halted with a jerk, and he pitched forward in his seat.

"We've lost power," Ruy said with a sharp intake of breath. His disembodied voice rose from the dark, shouting over the noise of sand raining sideways. "We're dead!"

"No, we're not," Landon said. "We have to get back. We can use the reserve tank for fuel."

"But we have to conserve that!" Ruy shouted back. "Without the GPS to guide us, we can't determine if we're headed in the right direction. Everything looks the same out there. We could go in circles until our reserves run dry."

"Move over," Landon said. "I'll drive."

"A-a-and wander aimlessly until we run out of air?" Ruy choked and gasped. "No, it's better to stay put for now."

"And do nothing?"

"S-surviving, that's something, isn't it? We have enough supplies in this rover for at least two weeks. We can only hope the winds won't last that long. Really, we don't know what to expect here."

Doc scoffed. "We have to go on. There's that trouble Chico mentioned."

"No b-bigger than ours."

"I'll tell you what," said Doc. "The wind, before it is through with us, will handle us like we are a toy. I say we go ahead, before the winds get worse. Let Landon drive. We started on the right course. How hard can it be to continue in a straight line? It can't be much farther." It was a command, of sorts, because without Inez, Doc held the highest rank.

Ruy grumbled and swished past Landon in the dark. A bench seat creaked as the geologist sank into it. Landon slid into the vacated driver's seat, then fingered the console until he felt the lever that triggered the reserve tank. "Let's get out of here," he said, flipping the switch.

But the switch jammed, and the engine remained dead. The controls, blank.

His muscles twitched as he opened a ground communications channel. "Torres, come in. Can you hear me?"

Static answered him, rather than Chico, and even though he'd expected no change in atmospheric interference, still he suffered another moment of anxiety.

"Where the hell are you, Torres? Come in, damn you."

Ruy spoke slowly from the back of the rover's cab. "This is more than a matter of too much dust in the atmosphere. Perhaps this disruption is something else. The...the disaster that message from the sphinx was trying to warn Earth about. It's here! It's all around us!"

Landon slammed his fist against the controls. He should've listened to Ruy's and Doc's warnings to leave the sphinx sooner. He was already responsible for the death of the captain, and now it appeared that he'd be responsible for the rest of their deaths as well.

He felt a hand on his shoulder. "It isn't your fault," Doc said.

His shoulders sagged. She was wrong. Psychic, maybe, but wrong.

The wind grew even stronger, or perhaps it sounded that way without competition from the engine. Sand scratched against the exterior. Howls and shrieks rose and fell in pitch. Landon lifted his chin. "Hear that? What's it sound like to you?"

"It's only the wind," Doc said cautiously, as if she were unsure of the correct answer. "What do *you* hear?"

A low rumbling noise rode along on the wind, growing in intensity and surrounding them with its vibration. Dread pushed Landon like a lead weight, deeper into his seat.

"Is it a...volcano?" Doc said.

"No," Ruy shouted. "There are two volcanoes in this immediate area, but they're long dead."

"Just like the planet, hmmmm?"

The rumble mushroomed to thunder, snuffing out the screech of the wind. Landon felt a vibration through his seat, and then the winds gusted with a shriek and caught them broadside. His stomach turned over. Ruy and Doc screamed as the rover shook and groaned and lurched sideways.

3

When Chico opened the pod doors, releasing the Thin Air Skimmer from the shuttlecraft, he was immediately sorry. Somehow, since deciding to leave the relative safety of base and struggling through ground winds in order to reach the buffeted shuttle—sometime in that interval, the storm had picked up several degrees of intensity.

It was more than wind, more than a fury of sand and dust. There must be demons in this maelstrom, black as night during the middle of day. Right now, it should be as bright on this planet as it could ever be under the half-warm light of a star that would burn itself slowly beyond the end of time.

Committed now, he pushed the stick forward.

He'd always thought these skimmers were like toys, and now he was sure of it, the way the wind took control and tossed it around. Picturing a paper airplane nose-diving into the ground, he pulled up. Hoping these were ground swells, praying that he could get above them, he clung to the controls. His entire arm vibrated from the strain of the little flying craft.

Some force stronger than his weight-trained muscles flicked his hand from the controls and took over. Encased in the small craft so that he was one with it, he felt himself turn end over end. The threat of nausea gripped him.

The stick shimmied only a few centimeters from his fingers, but he couldn't reach it. The monitor spun, his head spun, and he was going down.

Shit.

He couldn't remember why he'd disobeyed Masambwa, why he'd come out here, what he thought he had to prove. Uncle Jota would be pleased to learn about the death of Chico Torres. Hell, his uncle had probably sabotaged this craft and ordered up the dust storm.

His fingers trembled from the slow burn of rage. Why was it always the bitter, unloved men like Jota who managed to live the longest lives?

With that thought, the added, necessary strength flowed into his fingertips like a serum of virility, and he fought back.

He was never one to give up without a fight. He had more in common with his uncle than either of them cared to admit.

It helped to exhale slowly through gritted teeth, to think of this challenge as lifting. He couldn't let go now, or the weight would come crashing down on top of his head.

He wasn't going to think about the nausea.

His fingers touched the stick and clawed, wrapping around it. He pushed a little harder, wrestling the alien forces that whipped this godforsaken planet. Lucky for all of them he'd faithfully done his reps.

The craft righted itself, and he whooped as he pulled up above the worst of the wind. The force of the engine throbbed through the craft as it continued to climb, pressing him against his cocoon. Harder, and harder. Pain seared his head as the forces increased, but Chico grinned. He lived for flying.

A midday Proxima emerged from the murk, a welcome coal in the sky, and he had to shield his eyes from the suddenness of the ruddy glare. Beneath him, the sandy landscape shrank as the planet fell away. Above his head, the ring encircling the barren planet had an incandescent glaze to it, illuminated by the little sun at full power. He relaxed his grip and set his course to follow the ring east toward the sphinx mesa.

It was only then that he thought about having to go back down through the dust to find them on the surface. What if they'd left the sphinx already, and the rover, at this very minute, was struggling back across the plains?

No, they were more sensible than he was. Less impulsive.

"Rover, come in. Landon? Ruy? Doc? Do you copy? Can anyone hear me?" Then, as an after thought, he added, "Captain?"

4

Some obstacle slammed against the rover. The force of the impact caught the rover in its sideways lurch and righted it, tipping them back onto the balloon tires. Landon felt a moment of surprise that they still lived. Ruy and Doc screamed.

When the monstrous gale of wind finally eased, down to mere hurricane force, he toggled the jammed switch again. This time the reserve fuel tank engaged. The engine purred back to life. Doc cheered, and Ruy groaned.

Landon leaned against the controls, but the rover only rocked, as if it were stuck in its tracks. He felt a surge of hope. Perhaps the obstacle that held them in place was one of the boulders he'd likened to totem poles that formed a broken henge near their landing site. If so, they were almost home. Had the wind tumbled them so far? He put the rover into reverse and steered backwards far enough to clear the henge structure.

"What are you doing?" Doc said.

"Feeling my way." It was no different than the exercises he'd done hundreds of times when he'd moved through his *kata* with eyes closed.

With the GPS down, Landon could only guess that he was steering the rover around the edge of the henge. He knew the location where they'd planned to erect base relative to the shuttle and the henge. They slammed hard into something solid. The rover's engine died.

The headlights outside and the glow inside the cab winked out. Sand skittered against them in a continuous onslaught. It appeared as if they were buried. Blind.

As suddenly as the wind had hammered them, it eased now, rocking them in a gentle motion. Inside the cab, the murk lightened a degree. He could see Doc's face beside him. She reached for his hand, and it felt moist in his.

"It is...okay now, I think, yes?"

"It's letting up," Ruy said. "Listen."

"I don't hear anything."

"That's the point." Landon strained to hear the low whistles and murmurs of the fading wind. He peeled her fingers away from his hand and tried the engine again. It rattled and coughed, and then turned over with a steady hum. Again, he put the rover into reverse and steered around the blocking object. He couldn't be certain that the worst was over. If this was just a lull in the storm, then they needed to make haste.

Visibility increased to a couple meters. He could see far enough ahead to avoid a boxy obstacle that took shape in the gloom. And then another. He recognized them as crates they'd unloaded from the shuttlecraft, scattered by the wind, and he cheered softly.

"Look there," he said, pointing. "We made it." The bubbles of base loomed as two giant shadows ahead. No light shone through its viewports. It had lost power, or...

"It doesn't look like Chico's here," Ruy said, leaning over Landon's shoulder. "Perhaps the trouble he referred to was so bad that he had to abandon base. Something has gone seriously wrong."

Landon felt a burning sensation gnaw at his insides. He steered the rover close to the airlock of base and powered down the vehicle. Ruy and Doc let out nervous cries, somewhere between joy and sobs, as they snatched up canisters of oxygen and attached them to their suits.

"Come on, Landon, what are you waiting for?"

He refitted his helmet, hooked up a fresh tank to his suit, and followed them, squeezing into the airlock with the sample bucket. Despite the new hookup, the orange-red light still blinked inside his helmet. It should only take them a few minutes to cycle through, but it felt like hours as they waited for the precious air to cycle back into holding tanks. Finally, Ruy popped open the door and dropped out onto the rocky terrain, smoothed over by a fresh layer of dirt and sand. Puffs of dust arose from each crunching footstep as they bounded across the short distance from the rover to base. Landon hung back, watching Ruy and Doc leap toward the two interconnected bubbles of base, kicking up clouds of dirt and sand.

Suddenly, he felt as if there were no need for haste anymore. They had nothing but time. And time wasn't going to change the outcome for Inez. Nor for the alien whose bone he carried in the sample bucket.

"Landon?" Doc called over the suit-to-suit com. "Hurry up. We must not waste our air."

He forced himself to move forward, to follow the others. They crowded into base's airlock and sealed it up. Time slipped away as they waited for the recycled air to fill the chamber, the brushbot to vacuum the dust off their suits, the lights to turn green, the signal of readiness.

Always waiting.

Life had been reduced to a dependency on lights.

The lock released them into a small locker room. Doc stepped forward to the other door and peered through its porthole. "Chico finished this job by himself. We'd better check out life support systems before we enter."

Ruy studied a wall-mounted detector. "Carbon dioxide levels are at 0.121 psi. High concentration, but breathable."

"Are we sure the detector is working properly?" Landon stepped up beside Doc to look through the window into the

99

habitation module of what was to be their makeshift home. Shrouded by darkness and silence, it was filled with crates but empty of life. His shoulders slumped.

Ruy cleared his throat. "In any case, we cannot stay long in our suits. They need to go through the renewer."

"Let's go, then." Landon reached for the door latch, but Doc stopped him.

"We cannot risk contaminating the interior," she said. "We do not know what may be embedded in the joints of our suits that could not be vacuumed."

"This is a dead planet. Chances are that the dust is dead, too."

"A dead planet, yes. But we do not know what killed it. Perhaps a virus that has remained frozen—"

"Assuming the planet was alive to begin with," Ruy said.

Landon sighed. "Someone has to volunteer. It may as well be me." He popped the seal of his helmet and twisted it off, putting a merciful end to his warning light's nagging reminder that he'd failed Inez. They hadn't run a full battery of tests, but if life support had failed without setting off any alarms, then they'd all be dead soon, anyway. He inhaled deeply. The air smelled okay, only a little stuffy, and tangy new from its recent inflation.

More significant was that he still lived. No convulsions or nausea. Not even a headache. Quickly, he undid his suit, slithered out of it, and stepped through the door, closing it behind him. He stood inside the first module, which was to be their living quarters. This was the first time he'd entered these bubbles here on the planet, but he'd worked inside a similar model plenty of times during their training months in Goiás.

He felt transported back there to the Brazilian desert.

But this was different. This was the real thing. It smelled new, the way the SportDome had smelled that time he and Dad had had the first tour before any other outsiders had been invited inside. That was before vendors could stink it up with greasy foods, and before fans could make it old and used with urine, spit, and sweat.

And before the terrorist bomb that finished it, along with Dad. His world had changed then, as it was changing once again.

He blinked, and he was back on the planet again, surveying the curving perimeter wall where private bunk modules would stack once base was fully assembled. An oval table would occupy the central space for meals, conferences, and games. Now the inside of the bubble looked like a dome-shaped storeroom for crates, except for the single bunk that was assembled in the midst of this mess. Rumpled covers indicated recent use.

Landon shook his head and hurried through the connector into the second module. This was to be their work quarters, and it was equally dim and silent. Abandoned. Crates and unassembled chairs and tables were sorted according to the various workstations. Only the command center appeared to be up and running. Dumbbells and a little spray of sand sat at odd angles on the floor behind it, as if thrown there. Chico had been here, but he'd left in apparent haste.

Landon moved quickly to the command center. Lights were blinking from the console. A back-up system was keeping things running for now, but soon they'd have to hook up to the generator before stored power ran out, stopping the machines upon which their lives depended.

Always, the dependency on lights. One of them indicated a stored transmission, and he started to reach for it, eagerly, then stopped himself. The initials LW gave it the non-emergency tag of low priority, a personal message for Landon. He itched to queue it, but there was no time for that now.

He slipped into the command chair and started the systems check sequence, then studied the tracking screen. There was no blip to indicate the *Centaurus* was in range. The satellites were useless, off-line.

"All life-support systems check out," he said into his desk speaker. "You can come out now. Damage appears to be confined to the antennas—communications."

Ruy's voice came across the intercom. "Chico must have turned off the lights and then left. Because of the trouble?"

"The bigger question," said Doc, "is *where*. Where did he go?"

Landon turned to the sensor that tracked the whereabouts of functioning spacesuits, but no lights flickered. It was dead. "We can't do anything about him until after we've got full power back. Let's get to work."

5

Strapped into the pilot's seat of the skimmer, Chico was trying to remember why he'd left base in the first place. To save his skin, or some such nonsense. He laughed aloud. *Abuelita* had always warned him in her solemn, oh-wise-one voice to think things through before taking action.

His grandmother had been a gentler, more humane version of Masambwa. A visualization of the commander's somber face materialized in his head. She cared more about the damned rocks and dirt of this planet than the lives of her own crew. His veins tightened.

Either they would all leave this planet together, or they'd all die here together. Because a dead hero was better than a hero no one could believe in. Resolve pumped through his body as he studied the sandy shroud below.

The flight instruments indicated that his position in the skimmer was high above the sphinx mesa. He had to rely on the instruments, because down there, everything all looked the same. Surface contours remained hidden beneath the stirred-up sand and dust.

He shouted into his microphone. "Landon, can you hear me? You've got to get out of there now and get back to the shuttle. We have to lift off for rendezvous with the *Centaurus*, or else stay here forever."

But Landon didn't answer.

"Goddammit! Do I have to come down there and find you myself?"

Only static responded.

"Okay. I've got the skimmer, and I'm coming down." He scanned the mess below, searching for a more settled pocket where he might be able to maintain control all the way down.

Wait... What was that rising out of the dust ahead?

He looked again and saw his mistake. Nothing rose through the storm. Instead of something, it was nothing. It looked like a rip in the blanket of dust. A slice taken out of it. It was a dead spot in the storm, the eye of the storm. Not round like a hurricane's eye, but long and narrow. Okay, call it a cat's eye, but an eye all the same. If he found its exact center, he could navigate through it, the gateway through impassable turbulence. A grin tugged at his face.

Sure, he could do it. But then, how could he fight the winds to make it across the surface of the sphinx to find his friends?

Wait. Had he just thought of them as *friends*?

He set the program and felt the skimmer drop down toward the eye of the storm. The challenge ahead sent his spirits soaring as he circled lower. Then, the weight that kept him cocooned in place to the seat cushions suddenly vanished. Evaporated. For just an instant, he floated, as if nothing supported him at all.

Too soon, some force greater than Chico sucked away the floating sensation, and the bottom dropped out beneath him. His heart lurched up into his throat. A shot of nausea jolted through the pieces of lead that threaded through each cell of his entire body. He swore, but the words didn't escape his mouth.

None of this was anything new to him. He'd flown through disturbances before.

But this one felt different. Electrified. He felt himself shrink within a magnified current as the atmosphere split around him.

With the power of his will, Chico tried to lift the dead weight of his arm to access the controls. He couldn't do it. In that instant, he knew he was going to die. The instruments flickered, showing a hot spot ahead, where a pocket of air registered significantly warmer than anything else on this planet.

He could see it now. Something patchy ahead. Wispy, like...fog? No. Whatever this was, it was glowing and swirling with purplish sparkles. Galactically shaped, it rotated, drawing its wispy tentacles in spirals about its center. It was a miniature galaxy, only it lay within his reach. If only he could move his arm against the pressure. Weight thickened as if with the sum of universal matter, and he watched, helplessly, as the craft sped toward the bulls-eye center of the hot, glowing nebulosity.

Stars streaked past him in blazing lines of red, yellow, blue and white. Digits on the control panel blurred. His spine wanted to explode through the underside of the skimmer. He was a prisoner, plastered in position to watch death approach.

He felt the need to cross himself, but he couldn't move even the tips of his fingers. Pressure captured him in his cocoon. He wondered which way was up. Down must be the direction he was headed, but the surface of the planet failed to grow ominously before him.

His head wanted to split open from the pressure. He would grit his teeth, but he couldn't move his jaw against the pressure. This must be the way it felt, he decided, before death would take him in its welcome release from pain. But he wasn't ready to die, not with the promise of being a hero, even a postponed promise. The sacrifices he'd made would end up for nothing. His eyes filled with tears that pushed against his eyeballs instead of slipping down his cheeks.

All he could think of, as he approached death in that hot spot ahead, was that he'd failed. It hadn't been the civilians who'd fucked up. It had been himself.

Had he not had to prove his own worthiness to Uncle Jota, he wouldn't have been here in the first place. He would've stayed on Mars, remained a test pilot.

No, the big mistake was not telling the *Centaurus* the truth. Maybe Masambwa wouldn't have left them behind, had she known about Landon's story of the alien arm and the way the sphinx's mouth opened up and swallowed Pereira.

His mistakes were costing him his life, and while he could

accept the risk of death as part of his job, what he couldn't accept was dying first, before his crewmates...his friends. He was responsible for them. Something in his gut told him the others would die on this godforsaken planet without Chico. And for what?

He had to tell them. Warn them. If only he could reach the console with its switches controlling communications, then maybe he could get through to them on the skimmer's short-range channel. He raised his fingers, then lifted his arm. A few centimeters. Farther. They were *not* going to die. Fortunately for all of them, his weight-trained muscles overcame the forces working against him.

He opened his mouth, but only a gasp came out.

It was a struggle to make his mind work, to remember. The readings. The rising temperature. The energy field.

And then through a film of tears, he watched as unseen forces tugged at the purple galaxy, shifting its shape into a funnel, and he was falling into it. Layers of the concave sides peeled away in flapping sheets of purple. With each rip, a roaring sound filled his ears, his mind.

Tunnel... He gasped on the word as he plunged toward the center. Now a corridor of black stretched before him, and he stared at the black void with wide eyes. Had he gone blind? He was spinning, while opposing forces ripped at him. Then a slip of light appeared far away.

The light grew steadily wider, sweeping away the leftover wisps of dust. Pressure slowly eased. He reached the controls easily and steered the craft toward the light.

The light revealed that the surface of the planet was coming up fast. But... The landscape was no longer murky from the dust storm. It blazed under the full light of a yellow sun. So brightly yellow that it verged on white. His eyes ached.

There was no red anywhere from the half-dead daylight cast from the Centaurian triplets onto their planet. This place was not the same planet orbiting Proxima. Where in hell was he?

On the flat plains below, a giant beast crouched. It tilted its head upward, looking at him, showing its human face. Its mouth opened as if waiting for Chico to fall into its maw.

Dizzy, he spun closer.

Closer...

Until the spinning stopped with a sudden, jolting lurch. He smacked against something solid. Blackness folded around him.

Chapter Six

Smaller and shorter bursts of sand scratched across the exterior of the Mylar bubbles of base as the storm ebbed. Time slipped away from Landon as he worked to reestablish power, switching over from the emergency system that had supported their basic needs. Air. Indicator lights and bars flickered, stacking up maddeningly slowly as additional systems came back online with the return to full power.

Chico's suit had vanished from its plug-in stand in the closet. Once the sensor at Landon's console came back online to track the whereabouts of all of their suits, Chico's failed to register anywhere.

The sensor was functional, he knew, because its monitor displayed the dots of light that tracked Ruy and Doc, who searched outside for the pilot.

They returned inside with the report that they hadn't found him.

Landon, vaguely aware of his crewmates hovering behind his shoulder, continued to work. The others vacillated between their own jobs and monitoring him, which only made Landon feel all the more incompetent. He couldn't link the command center either to the *Centaurus* or to Chico. The transmitter at the console remained stubbornly quiet. The source of the disruption must be outside, somewhere in the antenna array.

But their pilot...? He'd vanished into the cloud of dust as effectively as had Inez.

Here inside the base, the air soon filled with thick smells of curry. The chain of command had fallen to Doc after Inez and Chico, and she assumed her new role of leadership by insisting they have a sit-down meal, their first since leaving the *Centaurus*. It wasn't right.

"Doctor's orders," she had said, prepping the food dispenser.

It chirped that the meal was ready before Landon could finish running the systems checks at the command center. Crates scraped against the plastic floor as Ruy dragged three of them around the sides of the oval table. Doc clattered utensils together and popped lids from trays of food.

"Dinner," she said-sang. "Come on, Landon."

They had to eat something more substantial than nutrition tablets. They had to go on. *He* had to go on. For Molly's sake.

The stored message would have to wait. Giving up on his blank transmitter for now, he crossed into the other module to the dinner table, but he angled his crate into a position that allowed him to see through the doorway between modules, to the blinking lights at the command center. He would be able to see if the transmitter came to life. He sank down onto his crate, cupping his forehead in the palms of his hands. He hadn't realized how tired he was. He couldn't look at the empty spaces at each end of the table, where Inez and Chico would've sat.

Doc placed a steaming plate next to his elbows. "Eat up. There's nothing we can do until the rover is ready to go out again, so you might as well eat in the meantime. Food will give us the strength we need to go back out there looking for Chico."

Strength. Yes, he needed that. He was too drained of life to think straight. He glanced at the plate. "What is it?"

She shrugged. "Tandoori lamb."

"Back at home, we called it soy." Ruy let out a long sigh. "We are never going to see home again."

Doc ticked her tongue and sat down next to Landon. "That's not true. We'll get there, one job at a time. Now, let's review what we've learned so far. I will start. The good news is that the shuttlecraft appears unharmed. We will have a way off this planet when the time comes."

"And the bad news," Ruy said, "is the open bay doors of number two skimmer."

"Chico must've gone out searching for us," Doc said between bites of her food.

"And now he is gone. Like the captain."

Another loss. Landon slouched lower on his crate. His sensoring machines should've connected him with Chico by now, in one way or another, even if the pilot didn't wish to report in. He was out there, somewhere. If he was in trouble, then the tracking devices would've located him.

They should've located Inez, too.

They had started as five in the landing party, and now they were three.

Doc nudged him. "Landon, your food is getting cold."

He looked up at her. What on earth was she smiling about? Didn't she realize he had no idea where to start looking for Chico? The pilot must've disabled the sensor in his suit. It was suicide.

"Go on," she said gently, "eat."

He stared down at his plate of lumpy brown sauce. They

couldn't start any more extensive search until after the rover recharged. It had used up all of its stored power, and there wasn't enough reserve fuel in their supplies to divert to the rover. If they used their reserves now, then that would be suicide, too, for the rest of them. If something went wrong on the return portion of their mission, they wouldn't have enough fuel to correct. He picked up his fork.

"What about the *Centaurus*?" Ruy said, stabbing at the lumps on his plate. "Why has it not shown up yet on your monitors?"

Stiffening, Landon glanced over at the command center. No new lights had appeared on the screens. The blip that would've indicated the ship in its orbit still hadn't materialized. He scowled. Maybe there was something else he'd missed.

"It's just out of range," Doc said.

Ruy shook his head. His voice quavered. "Chico told us there was trouble and that we had to return immediately to base. We did not, and now the ship is g-gone."

Landon lifted his chin and glared at the geologist. "Gone? Gone, how?" His daughter was up there.

"That is the question, is it not? I suspect it crashed onto the planet. Possibly, it left without us. Either way, we are on our own."

"*Non.* It is nothing like that. We lost communication, that is all. The dust storm, yes?" Doc's voice rose to a shrill cry, and Landon wondered if all three of them were suffering negative aftereffects of cryogenics.

He waved his fork in the direction of the command center. "The ship doesn't show up on the monitors because the antennas must've suffered some damage. I'll go back outside to work on them as soon as the suits are done renewing. Don't worry, the ship is still up there. It has to be, because it's far enough above the atmosphere that the storm wouldn't have affected it."

His fork clattered onto his plate as he gazed over at the nearest viewport. Pieces of lavender sky showed through lingering wisps of dust. His daughter was up there, too. Not only Molly but also the only remaining tachcom within four light years. He wondered if the tachcom could send messages to the past, before the dust storm had messed up everything. Tachyonic transmission, after all, was nothing more than time travel.

It would be useless. Without a proper receiver on the other end, any attempt to communicate with the past would be nothing more than a bunch of lost tachyons spinning aimlessly through the universe.

But there must be something he could do. He took a deep breath and saw his own hand before him. Slowly, he slipped his thumb between his first and second fingers and studied the *figa* his fist made. As the alien's hand had made, trying to emerge from the sphinx's mouth.

The *figa*, a good luck symbol. But it hadn't worked. It hadn't brought Inez or the rest of them good luck on this mission.

The human *figa* had emerged from the alien tomb *before* Inez had fallen into it, disappearing from all detection devices. As if she'd fallen through a gate of some sort, a gate to the remote past where she could teach aliens about the *figa*...

He shook his head, unable to believe the wild thoughts tumbling through his mind. Maybe Doc was right about those hallucinations.

He became aware that their voices had stilled, and they

were frowning at his hand. All sounds had died except for the swishing sounds of the ventilation system. He untangled his fingers and used his hand to reach for his fork. He studied the soy strips on his plate, smothered in a dark sauce. They appeared charbroiled, but they weren't.

Ruy and Doc watched him silently for several heartbeats, and then Ruy picked up where he'd left off. "You are the one who spoke to Chico," Ruy said, looking at Doc, ignoring Landon. "That is what he said, correct? Trouble."

Doc's voice returned to its low level of soothing, as if trying to calm a hysterical child. "We don't know what kind of trouble he meant."

"They crashed," Ruy said, "and he went out looking for survivors."

"They did not crash," she said patiently.

But Ruy wouldn't give up. "Then Chico was looking for *us*, and I can guess why. When he was doing the inventory, setting up base for us, he must have discovered that we have less life support remaining than we thought we had. Because of the storm, he could not tell us about it over the com, and so he had to go out and find us personally. To tell us that we all had to leave." Ruy grew more animated as he talked, and then he turned to Landon. "You said it yourself. The indicators and detectors are still not functioning properly. We do not have three months of life support. Maybe only three hours."

"Could that be true, Landon?" Doc said, her voice rising again. "You're the machine expert."

Landon rubbed his head, where he felt the first aching throbs of a headache. "It's true that things are not up and running properly yet, and it's true that we haven't heard from the *Centaurus* yet, but we surely have more than three hours of life support."

"All may not be lost," Ruy said quietly. "There are still the emergency cryo-tanks we can use."

"Only as a last resort." Doc turned to Landon. "You're sure the problem is on this end?"

He shook his head.

"They'll send another mission here to rescue us," Ruy said.

Landon rose from the table and carried his plate to the washer bin. If they were forced to use the tanks, that was death for sure. They couldn't count on a possible future mission to rescue them. "We need to wait for the rover to finish recharging, and then get back out there, looking for Chico."

"We either die now," Ruy said, "or we go into the cryo-tanks to die later."

"No, we're not going to die." Landon stalked across the module to peer out the viewport. The silhouette of the shuttlecraft showed like a bird at rest a hundred meters away. The dust had lifted enough that he could go out there and recover what he could of the antennas. "There's a way out of this."

"If we have to use the cryo-tanks to await rescue by some future mission," Doc said, "then we should consider conserving our remaining life support for that time. We might need it then, to give us the necessary time to get off the planet and rendezvous with the rescue vehicle."

Landon turned away from the view and crossed the module to the suit closet. "It's too soon to give up."

"What difference does it make now?" Ruy said. "They are gone. All of them."

Doc huffed. "I do not take kindly to losing my patients.

I have lost one already today, possibly two. I will not lose anymore. Where do you think you're going, Landon?"

"Right now, to work on the antennas. Then we're going out, and we'll rescue Chico first. After that, we'll go back to the sphinx to keep searching for Inez."

"Perhaps you are right," Doc said, nodding. "Their deaths will not be finished until they're recovered and brought home. We'll reduce their remains, of course. It's simply disrespectful to leave them behind."

"We also have to recover my tachcom parts while we're there. If I can assemble a tachcom down here on the surface, then it'll solve all these issues we're having with communication."

Doc pointed at Ruy. "And you must complete the analysis of the samples we brought back, yes?"

2

As Landon worked outside, reassembling the antennas, he felt Doc's eyes on him. From time to time, he looked up and saw her shadowy outline against the windows of light pouring out of base. It was a good feeling, being watched. He wasn't alone on an alien planet.

He tried not to think about Ruy's fears, but they niggled the back of his mind as he guzzled oxygen from the new canister he'd hooked into his suit. He felt as if he was using wasteful amounts, but it wasn't as if they could conserve a thing like oxygen. Ruy had given up hope, but that was wrong. Landon would prove it before rising hysteria endangered the mission further.

He scavenged wind-tossed pieces and repaired the antenna

array with the bin of spare parts that he'd brought outside with him. Finally, Doc's shadow at the viewport held up a thumb. He'd done enough.

After cycling back inside and putting away his suit, he headed straight to the command center with its blinking lights. Everything seemed to be hooking up, but still, the transmitter's screen remained blank.

"Conference in ten minutes," Doc called out.

Landon eyed the dot of light that indicated the stored radio transmission still waited for him. He tapped the screen, queuing the transmission to play. Finally, he had a chance to view it while he waited for the systems checks to finish running.

The screen flickered, then words scrolled across, verifying that this was a personal message for Dr. Landon Walker. Traveling at the speed of light, it had taken more than four years to catch up to the *Centaurus*. Point of origin was Goiás headquarters of the International Space Agency. An image of the white buildings of the compound against the backdrop of Brazilian desert took Landon back there, to the days of his training, along with a flood of memories.

Sam Talcott, promoted officially to director and looking at least a decade more subdued than the bear-like figure Landon remembered, resolved on the screen. He was thinner now—or at least, four years ago—and more salt than pepper streaked his hair, thinned to wisps around a bald crown. Landon felt a lump thicken in his throat.

Sam frowned and looked down at a crumpled piece of paper he held in one hand. Just like H.F. and his bits of papers. Sam had apparently picked up the habits of the man he'd replaced, Landon's mentor, H.F. Washington, whose remains awaited in cold storage for possible reconstruction one day, if technology ever caught up to the task. H.F. had been the eccentric genius behind the initial organization of ISA, who'd found the funding for Landon's tachyonic research, and who'd pulled Landon into this mission long ago. No one was a big enough man to follow in H.F.'s footsteps, and Landon resented Sam for even trying.

"Greetings," Sam said, a voice from the past, and then swallowed hard, "in case you survived. We haven't told the public that we lost contact with you somewhere in the Oort Cloud. We don't want to alarm them unnecessarily, considering the..." He paused and then coughed. "Considering the 'artifact' you discovered in Patagonia, under that glacier. And thanks to your sister, news of that discovery has leaked out. So the public is already on edge. Aliens are the new terrorists." He broke off with a chuckle, and the sound of it sent a bad taste sliding down the back of Landon's throat.

"Naturally," Sam continued, "we did not inform your sister this time about the bombardment you endured in the Oort Cloud. She thinks you're still on course. Hell, maybe you skated through somehow. In that case, she wants—no, she *insisted* on sending you a message. She's transmitting from our office at the Holland Annex, and then our techies will paste all this together. But before I sign off, in case you ever receive this, I would remind you of your prime objective, to track the emission the aliens sent, to find their nest, to root them out of hiding. We'll do the rest from here."

Landon stiffened in his seat. The sound of hostility in Sam's voice sent an electric bolt charging through him. What did Sam mean? What did he think he could "do" from Earth?

The screen flickered and switched to an image of a woman

whose gaze darted nervously around the blank room in which she sat, hunched over. She couldn't be his sister, Greer, who spent hours fussing over her cosmetics and the latest fashions. This woman's face was free of paint. Her flesh puffed under her eyes and wrinkled across her brow. Her hair hung in uncombed, pale clumps.

"Is this thing on?" she said, looking off-screen. She *was* Greer. He recognized her irreverent tone of voice.

She narrowed her eyes to hardened nuggets and leaned closer to her camera, whispering. "Okay, so if you're out there, and if you can hear this, then I thought you should know."

He braced himself. Know what?

She fidgeted some more, but then his sister had always fidgeted. Her overly active nervousness had always landed her in trouble, but there was something different about her now. Something missing from her demeanor. She had lost the spark of her special joy that drove her through life. She seemed defeated. Scared.

"I hope you're treating my niece well, Landie, 'cause you know how you can be sometimes, so absorbed in your all-holy work that you forget about everyone else around you."

He opened his mouth to protest, but then caught himself, remembering that she wasn't really sitting in front of him. This wasn't a two-way conversation.

She stopped and pulled back, tensing, as if listening and looking for something. Or for someone? Whatever it was, it failed to materialize, and she leaned low again.

"Give her a hug for me. You will, won't you? Even though the courts gave her custody to me, I still think she's better off with her daddy. So you're taking good care of her for me, aren't you?"

He squirmed in his seat. His sister knew the arrangement: Molly was to remain in cryo-sleep for the duration of this voyage. Why was she ignoring the fact? Why didn't she get on with whatever it was that she wanted him to know?

"Well, it turns out that it's probably a good thing she's with you, instead of with me, because..." She looked around again.

He wanted to shout at her to go on, and then a voice murmured something to her off-screen. She dipped her chin in a nod and went on, lowering her voice in a rush of words that tumbled out in one long breath.

"It's not really safe here anymore, Landie, ever since that crazy woman tried to kill me in Patagonia, and now her friends are after me, all the way over here in the Annex, and I think they followed me here in their little box-drawer wormholes, but don't worry about it, because you wouldn't understand." She gasped for air, and then plunged on. "Just so you know, they're after me, but I think what they really want is Molly, and I also think that they think she's here with me, because she used to be, but she's not now, thank goodness. I know you don't believe me, 'cause you never do, but it was only the other day when I was heading over to the ISA office here in the Annex, minding my own business, and some car went off the rails and missed hitting me by centimeters. See? They thought Molly was with me. Why do they want to kill her? You know, don't you? And that's why you wanted to take her with you. But that's not all. Now, you'd better sit down for this next piece of news. Remember that glacier in Patagonia and what we found underneath it? Well, your friends at ISA went in there to excavate after you left on the *Centaurus*, and you know what they found? Are you ready for this? They found *nothing*. Nothing like what you told them about. They didn't even find Summer. Her body wasn't there."

She prattled on for a while longer, but he wasn't listening anymore. The transmission ended, and the screen before him went as blank as his understanding.

He had been with Summer when she'd died inside that ancient alien spaceship under the glacier. She'd died in his arms before he'd had to flee with Molly for their lives. They'd had no choice but to leave Summer's body behind.

It was there. It had to be.

3

Landon wasn't sure how long he sat there, dazed. The transmission screen in the center of the command console was a blank rectangle. Other lights danced around its periphery as Greer's words replayed in his mind. Finally, he became aware that Doc was calling to him, for how long she'd been calling he wasn't sure. She summoned him to the oval table, now converted to a conference table. Three steaming mugs sat at their places.

Trying to process the questions fogging his mind (Was Greer delusional? Did someone want to kill Molly? What happened to Summer? And to the alien spaceship under the glacier?), he staggered across the module and sank down onto his crate, interrupting Ruy in the middle of what sounded like a speech.

"Glad you could join us," Doc said, looking up at him with a smile that wasn't happy. "Ruy was just beginning to tell us what he's learned so far about that rock sample you found and hauled back with us from the sphinx."

Ruy cleared his throat and continued. "The predominant theory asserts that there is a window of opportunity in the early days of planetary formation, when conditions are favorable to the emergence of life. We now know that it's more likely to close before life can evolve on terrestrial planets such as this one—"

"Wait a minute," Landon said, coming alert, clearing the mud from his mind. "What are you suggesting? About *life*?" He meant the Tititri. Had Ruy found them?

"Let him finish," Doc said.

Ruy's thumb stroked the handle of his mug. He kept talking, as if unaware of the presence of the other two. "Along with the planet's small size and its heavy bombardment, which created all the craters we see, it couldn't retain enough carbon dioxide during its outgassing phase to maintain a high enough temperature, and as the planet cooled, it lost its atmospheric pressure as well."

Landon couldn't explain the hand he'd seen emerge from the sphinx's mouth, but he suspected it had belonged to a Tititri, displaced by some catastrophe and brought here by some anomalous means of travel—maybe a wormhole, as his sister had mentioned, comparing it to a drawer. He'd assumed she'd made it up, as she usually did, but—

He chided himself. He was disbelieving her story as much as Ruy and Doc doubted his own story of the hand.

"Its oceans vaporized," Ruy continued, "but the thinning atmosphere couldn't retain water vapor, so it escaped and was lost to space. In essence, the planet died, along with whatever life may have been evolving on its surface at the time."

"Oceans?" Landon said.

Ruy stopped talking and blinked at Landon. "You yourself have seen the evidence to support the presence of oceans here at one time. You mapped runoff channels in your survey from orbit, remember?"

"They were rivers, sure. But, *oceans*?" Could the Tititri have been *indigenous* here?

"There are enough oxides locked up in the samples I've examined that support the theory of vast amounts of water," Ruy said. "And now there's the sample we retrieved."

"*We*?" Landon leaned forward, coming up off his seat, ready to pounce. It still irritated him the way Ruy had frozen up back there, driving the rover away from the sphinx.

Doc laid a restraining hand on Landon's arm. "Yes, what about that sample?" she asked.

Landon scraped his hand across the stubbles of his beard and settled back down, reaching for his mug. He sipped the bitter brew, one of Doc's restorative teas, and memories of the shaman's brew high in the mountains of Patagonia washed over him.

"Just a minute," Ruy said. "I'm getting there. I'm no biologist. Too bad ISA didn't sign one on to this mission."

"That's me," Doc said with a scowl. "Just tell us about the sample. It looks more like a rock than a plant."

Ruy sighed. "It's neither. Its composition is simple quartz, you see, but there's something else. I never would've believed it if I'd not seen it with my own eyes. But it was clear. Too clear in the samples I shaved off. Without a doubt, what I saw were the rudiments of cell structure. Feel free to check my observations, if you don't believe me. But in my opinion, it's unquestionably a petrified bone." His voice dropped to a murmur. "It must've been the water from ancient oceans, filtering through the sand, that petrified it." He shook his head again. "Perhaps the seismic disturbance we experienced in the morning unearthed it, so to speak."

Landon set his mug down with a thud, splattering him with drops of hot liquid. So. He'd been right. It really was a *bone*. A Tititri bone. "When do you believe this petrifaction occurred?"

Ruy shrugged. "Samples I've taken and measured suggest a solidification age of four and a half billion years. Cratering models, however, date back to just over three billion years. Around the time stromatolites inhabited the Earth."

"So what are you suggesting? He died three billion years ago?"

"We will have to wait for Dr. Montague to run her tests."

"Which will wait," Doc said, "until after I see to the health and well-being of my patients. Have some more tea."

Landon shoved his mug away. "But you must have an idea."

The corners of Ruy's mouth turned down, and the tips of his protruding ears flamed red. "No, that would be assuming too much. I really cannot say." He picked up his mug and brought it to his lips. "However, I can tell you this much. This petrified bone is obviously from a highly evolved being. It's far older than any such life we've seen on Earth."

Yes, of course. The Tititri had lived here, little more than four light years from Earth, a mere pebble toss in galactic measures. If Ruy were right, and their window of favorable conditions for life had been open only a short time, they wouldn't have had enough time to evolve into their higher form.

Then, they'd come from someplace else. They hadn't evolved here.

Because they had been too highly evolved, both physically and intellectually, to have reached that evolutionary point in the short window of time when life could live on this planet.

He wondered if they'd come here originally because they'd

been chased here. Maybe by their enemy, the Zyvors. He'd learned back in the alien spaceship that no longer existed under the glacier in Patagonia that the Zyvors wanted the Tititri dead, for whatever reason.

Once the Tititri came here to this planet, escaping the Zyvors, they'd built that sphinx with a human-simian head atop the body of an animal. Maybe that animal had been the indigenous life form found here. The head indicated that the space-faring settlers here were humanoid. Cousins to humanity. And then, once the Zyvors found them here, the already space-faring Tititri sent a scoutship, looking for a new home on Earth, where they reached out to their cousins—humans. Only to expose Earth and all of humanity to the Zyvor war. Maybe they were the ones who'd taken Summer's body. He shivered.

"It's the time line that troubles me," Landon said, trying to find a way to tell them about the Tititri without betraying his promise to them. "Life didn't develop here on its own. How could it in a triple star system like this? No. They came here from somewhere else."

"From Brazil?" Doc said, sending pointed glances at his hand. He'd made a *figa* out of it before. "Is that what you're thinking?"

He didn't know what he was thinking. He wasn't sure that he even *could* think. It seemed so hard to pull his thoughts together into anything that made sense. Maybe it was true, what Doc had suggested about hallucinations following cryo-sleep.

It all had to do with time *and* space. If Ruy could date the bone more precisely, and if Brandt, the astronomer on the ship, could calculate where in space this planet had been at that time—

when the catastrophe with the Zyvors occurred, petrifying the Tititri remains—then Landon could direct the astronomer to aim the shipboard tachcom at that point in time *and* space.

Before Landon could sort out his tangle of thoughts, Doc nudged him. "While we wait for the rover to be ready, we will review the events leading up to Inez's accident. You have downloaded the recording from your suit, yes?"

Grateful for a distraction from the puzzle, he nodded and flipped the table screen up from its protective casing. Crates creaked as Ruy and Doc shifted their positions behind him. Landon tapped in his instructions and brought up the recording. They were wasting time, waiting for the rover, but they had no other choice if they wanted to travel very far. How far had Chico made it in the skimmer? They needed to be out looking for him.

They settled back with their tea to watch what Landon's suit had seen. He sped up the replay of their first steps on the surface of the planet, but after that, Doc instructed him to slow the video to real time. He suspected she was looking for inconsistencies in his story. They watched in alternating fast and slow spurts as Landon and Inez constructed the platform lifter and trekked across the sphinx, until the moment of the first seismic disturbance that shook the ground.

And then the screen went blank.

Landon swore under his breath and reached for the touchpad. "That's funny... What happened to it?"

Doc harrumphed. "We need to see the events immediately preceding the accident that claimed Inez."

"Yes, I know," he said. "It recorded. Must be something wrong here. Somewhere. Give me a minute." He continued to search, but it was as if the rest of the corder's file had disappeared into the ether.

He was aware of Doc and Ruy behind him, watching him silently suspicious as he searched for the missing remainder. It must be here. But it wasn't.

He swiped the top of his buzz-cut head. "There was this purple aurora—"

"Impossible," Ruy said, slurping his tea. "Without a magnetic field, there can be no aurora."

"What did I see, then? It looked like streaks of purple, flapping across the sky."

"An anomaly, perhaps, but not an aurora."

"Okay, then, it was an anomaly. It ripped open the sky above our heads as well as the ground beneath our feet."

Ruy shook his head.

"Look, do you want to know or not? You asked what happened, and if the suit vid won't show you, then I have to tell you."

Doc rested her hand on Landon's and said, "Yes, please go on."

"Maybe it couldn't happen," Landon said, "but it did." He described how he'd been standing atop the rim of the canyon, speaking to Chico on the link when the canyon wall split apart beneath his feet. He'd watched, trying to describe it to Chico, as debris rained down, covering Inez, and it was as if Inez had been glued to her spot, unable to break free. In fact, Landon himself had felt some sort of pull when later, he'd watched the bottom of his excavated hole rip apart, and a force had tried to prevent him from moving, but he'd managed to overcome that force, breaking free.

A noise crackled in the other module. Landon looked up

from the conference table, where his suit's vid had stopped playing. Over at the command center, the transmitter was coming to life.

He sprang from his crate and leaped through the doorway connecting the two bubbles of base. His crewmates pounded close behind, their heaving breath tickling the back of his shoulder.

"*Centaurus* to base, come in please," said a steely voice amidst the static spitting out of the transmitter. "Masambwa here. Do you copy?"

Landon reached the desk first. His thumbs shook with relief as he pressed them down onto the controls. "Roger, we copy. Good to hear your voice, commander. What's your status?"

"Orbit is still decaying."

Her words sent spikes through him. Molly was up there.

"Where's Torres?" Masambwa continued. "He should have told you." She squinted at her screen, apparently observing Doc and Ruy who leaned behind Landon's shoulder.

Landon felt as if his air supply had just cut off. "Ah... We haven't talked to him yet. We've had a few problems of our own down here." He should report the situation, and he *would*. But first, he had to know about his daughter's situation. "What about your orbit?"

"Energy burst. Presumably from the planet's surface. Pulled us out of orbit."

Her description spun through his mind. Had it been a larger-scale version of the same force that had tried to pull him through the bottom of the hole he'd excavated over at the sphinx's mouth? He felt Doc's fingers clutch the back of his shoulder. Ruy gasped in his ear.

Masambwa went on, her voice devoid of emotion. As if she were giving a casual report. "At this rate, we anticipate intersecting the plane of the ring in approximately twelve more hours. Impossible to predict how much sooner than that we will start encountering countless collisions with the ring's particles. We cannot risk the likely damage to the ship that we are sure to sustain. Therefore, we are proceeding with plans to re-ignite the engines and pull away. We will depart for approximately ten days to acquire additional fuel."

"Fuel?" Doc said. "From where?"

"Proxima Centauri. It's a relatively simple procedure."

"But there has to be enough fuel." Landon frowned. "They wouldn't have sent us here in the first place if we didn't have enough." H.F. had pushed the mission hard, eager to get it off the ground. Masambwa had gone along with him, assuring that there was enough fuel in their supplies. Apparently, there hadn't been. And yet, she had agreed to proceed.

"It will be enough," Masambwa said coldly, "after I top off our supplies."

Something else had malfunctioned, Landon thought. It had started with his equipment.

"But the ship," Ruy said, "is not equipped for helium diving."

"Brandt is re-programming the exterior scoops. Would you rather stay down there forever, doctor?"

"N-no, ma'am."

"I thought not. There will be only minimal risk of exposure to us. The shelter chamber will protect us from solar rays. We'll be working from within it."

"Molly!" Landon clenched his fist. "What about Molly?"

Masambwa's cool gaze fell onto him, as if her force of will

could push him back from the screen. "Yes. The child. We have not forgotten her. Brandt is with her now, preparing her for our move into the shelter."

"But you can't move her cryo-tank."

"Of course not, doctor. Brandt has begun awakening procedures."

Chapter Seven

Night had fallen, and the *Centaurus* appeared as a new star, blazing to life in the heavens overhead as she fired her engines. Landon felt his throat tighten. He peered through the rover's window at the dot of light that carried Molly, his baby girl. She was awake now, far out of his reach, and at the mercy of the alien who controlled her.

He watched her course across the sky as her light faded, and finally he could see her no more. She had left orbit.

His heart ached as he continued to stare at the spot in the dark sky where the ship's light had been. Luckily, Ruy was driving the rover, which gave Landon the opportunity to focus elsewhere. That left Doc as their navigator. Finally recharged, the rover rolled back across the sea of sand toward the sphinx. Along the way, there was no sign of a crushed skimmer. No pinging sounds. No red dot that tracked Chico's suit.

The only sounds came from the thrum of the rover's engine as they swayed and lurched through the fresh deposits of sand. Landon felt grateful that there was no idle chatter, not as Inez had challenged him with her barrage of questions about his failures when they'd first crossed this distance to the sphinx. The silence told him that his crewmates must feel as hammered as he felt. Less than two days ago—a lifetime ago—the five members of the landing party had entered the shuttlecraft with high anticipation and then detached from the *Centaurus*. Now they'd been reduced to three survivors, battered and lonely.

When the mesa loomed before them, its size no longer filled Landon with a sense of wonder. This was merely a job he had to do, and he dreaded it. He played the rover's light beams across the base, but they found no skimmer. Perhaps it had landed on top. Chico had bantered about performing that feat. They would have to scale the mesa's walls, looking for him, returning to the site of Inez's accident, returning to the entrance into the sphinx. He knew it was there. He'd seen it.

However, the platform lifter was not. It had vanished in the storm.

2

When Chico opened his eyes, the first thing he noticed was that he was still alive. Pain tore through his left arm like a searing cutting beam. Instantly, he relaxed the muscle, allowed the arm to hang limply in his lap. He squinted through the open place where the skimmer's windshield had once been.

"*Madre*," he whispered.

A funnel had swirled out of the dust storm and sucked him through a black tunnel, streaked with colorful lights, and they'd fallen, he and his skimmer, as if through a gyrating kaleidoscope amongst tumbling color, towards a distant pinprick of light, widening like a spreading stain until he emerged into the blazing light of a sunny day. Where the monstrous sphinx greeted him with open jaws.

He couldn't see it anymore.

Had he dreamed up that black tunnel in the instant before

impact? Was he dead now?

No, the pain felt too sharp. Too real.

His skimmer had crumpled against a dark, gray rock wall. Somehow it had landed right side up, but it was as useless as his arm. All that separated him from the elements of this rabbit hole place where he'd ended up was the flexifabric of his suit. A fresh suit—an undamaged suit—started with six hours of life support unless an extra canister of oxygen was attached. He hadn't brought one along, thinking he wouldn't need the extra time.

Wincing, he lowered his gaze to the suitpac on his right arm. The small computer that could analyze his suit's systems had been installed there because he was a lefty. But what was the use now without his left arm? The engineers hadn't thought of everything. He started to chuckle, but it hurt.

At least the display lights in his helmet hadn't started their final countdown yet, warning him of low oxygen. But then, how could he be sure that his suit was properly functioning? Maybe life support would run out and he'd never know it was the last breath of oxygen he'd draw.

It'd be better that way. *Virgen María, madre de Dios*, let it be that way.

His gaze shifted to the wall of rock rising up out of the skimmer's nose. He whistled. The air was clear, although shadowy dark. And eerily still. No wind. No dust.

It must've been his imagination that had led him to believe he'd seen what he'd seen: a sunny, blue sky that shone a Mother-Earth blue, compliments of a thick atmosphere. A crouching monster of an animal. It hadn't been real, he realized now, after the fact. It had been a statue. Like the sphinx.

No. It *was* the sphinx. But it was different, somehow. Which meant this had to be another time. Another place.

That was crazy. Craziness...that's what had lost him his control of the craft.

With his clumsy, right arm, he fumbled with the catch of his harness, released it, then groped in front of him to open a channel for communications. "Mayday, mayday. Skimmer II to anyone. Do you copy? Hell!" Communications had been out for hours. Why should he expect anything to change now?

Reaching across his body, he pushed against the hatch and yelped with pain. Fucking jammed. His right arm was as useless as the left one. An even bigger pain wrestled with his head. Just his luck that it was his *left* arm that got broken. Or mashed in its socket. Or severed from his body. He wondered if his suit was filling up with his own blood, and the thought made him dizzy.

The rocky wall started to spin slowly before him.

Why had he thought he could rescue the civilians with a skimmer? He'd let his emotion get in the way. The *abuela* was right. He'd been born with only half a set of brains. With not enough strength left to hold up his head. He slumped in his seat. Nothing to do but wait for death.

No!

He breathed slowly, deeply, and felt the serum of virility flow through his veins, trickle that it was. He couldn't give up. Not now. He was a hero. He had to remember that. Slowly, he reached out with his good, clumsy arm, groped for the control panel before him, and felt the touchpad that would release the flare. His eyes couldn't be trusted. He knew his flying machines by touch better than anyone.

Found it. Felt his own strength escape like a slow leak through a puncture in some pressurized thing. Wrapped his fingers over the pad.

Pushed.

Nothing.

Harder.

He winced when he heard the flare escape like a bullet, rocketing up and over the rim of the rock wall.

Post-crash stress syndrome, that's what was fooling him into believing he'd seen...a blue sky...and the sphinx.

3

Suited up and under a canopy of floodlights, Landon worked outside the rover, mounting the grapnel gun to its tripod. Ruy and Doc hovered behind him, believing they assisted, but they were only getting in his way. The device would do all the work, once he got it set up. It came loaded with several hundred meters of roping.

"Are you sure this rigging will be safe for climbing in the dark?" Ruy said through the helmet-to-helmet link.

"Landon has tested it before, yes?"

"Roger that." Landon glanced over at Ruy. Fear gleamed through the geologist's faceplate. "This won't be as comfortable as the platform lifter, but with a little work on our part, it'll get us to the top, all the same." He made the final adjustments for guidance of the missile-like grapnel, then fired.

The curving trajectory disappeared into the darkness outside the spotlight's beam. The grappling hook would lodge somewhere up there among the rocky ledges of the sphinx, close to where he'd installed the platform lifter before the storm. A shower of pebbles rattled back at them. Ruy yelped and lunged backwards, closer to the rover. Landon held his breath, expecting the grapnel to come tumbling after the pebbles, but when the dust settled, the roping hung firm.

"It's ready," he said, clamping harnesses onto the rope. "Let's go rock climbing."

The climb was straight up in places, sometimes lit by the spotlight from below, and other times in deep darkness, with only his helmet light to show the way. He controlled the mechanism through his harness, and the rope did most of the work. Still, he had to guide it, groping with his boots to feel the incline. The occasional rock climbing he'd done in British Columbia with his father had never prepared him for this, many years older, encumbered by the awkwardness of his gear. The shell of his flexisuit held him farther away from the rock than what felt comfortable. His balance shifted with the extra mass of the canister of oxygen strapped to his back. Time and again, he needed to pause and readjust. Each time he stopped on a dark ledge, Doc whined into his helmet. Harnessed behind him, she demanded he move back into the spotlight's track where she could follow him easier.

Resting, he shut her out with the force of his mind, flicked off his helmet light, and twisted his neck upward to scan the heavens. Proxima, where Molly was headed, was not visible in this night sky. Instead, the crystal brilliance of Earth's sun glittered from Cassiopeia.

He thought of the times he'd taken Molly to the observatory on SpaceHab...it seemed so long ago, almost as if his memory was that of another person. For Molly...space was her future...

"Landon, answer me!"

"Relax, I'm still here," he said.

Doc's voice shrilled inside his helmet. "Your blood pressure is elevated, and—"

"Looks like there's a fissure here." He didn't want to hear anymore of his medical details, which she kept throwing at him, just because she could monitor them from her specially equipped med suit. "The fissure runs up the side of the wall. We'll follow it up."

"Something the quake opened up?" Ruy said, climbing below Doc.

Landon turned his helmet light back on. "You would know about quakes better than me."

"Well, watch your step, yes?" Doc said.

The fissure opened onto another ledge, and he guided the roping to it. He paused the mechanism to stand for a moment on semi-level ground. He must be close to the top. The rover looked like a toy below, parked beside the spotlights.

He stepped carefully along the ledge. His harness clamped onto the rope, holding him securely, but leaving his feet free. He gripped the rope so tightly that his arms ached. His helmet's spot swept along the ledge before him. Something obstructed the way. Rocks had slid down from the upper rim, blocking his access to the rest of the ledge. Still thinking of Molly, he stumbled into the field of rocks.

And immediately, he slipped.

His arms flailed out, and he bounced against rocks of all sizes. The rope caught him before he could fall very far, and he recoiled into emptiness. Rocks crunched and moved beneath him, sliding down, and when his boot touched again, briefly, he sprang away from the slipping rocks.

"Oh, shit!" Doc screamed in his helmet, and he tore his gaze away from the ledge, where he was attempting to regain his balance.

He'd triggered a rockslide.

Tumbling, crashing, roaring rocks. One final thud. The floodlights shining up the side of the rock wall winked out. And then silence.

4

Chico floated, caught somewhere in the netherworld of semi-consciousness. Scraping, whirring sounds scuffled around the perimeter of his awareness. Murmuring voices.

Voices?

He felt so...nothingly numbed.

Voices?

His brain slogged into a semi-aware state, crunched under the weight of the universe. Yes, he recognized the susurrant sounds as voices. But he didn't understand them. Until... A screech broke loose. A woman's squeal. Funny, how women alone could reach that unique pitch.

"Chico? Is that you? It *is* you. Oh my god!"

Fingers jostled him, shaking his cheek. He struggled to lift his eyelids from the glue that stuck them together. Light seared into him. A face bent close to his. An unhelmeted, woman's coppery face, framed with dark curls. Inez.

"Let's get you out of here," she said. Then she turned her face away from his and spoke to someone else, uttering the chirping, sing-songy sounds of a language like nothing he'd ever heard.

5

Landon stood frozen atop the sphinx's head, gasping from his climb. He stared down at the sea of sand—a sea of black now, in the aftermath of the rockslide.

Doc cried softly next to him.

Ruy collapsed to his knees. "What do we do now? We have no way back to base without the rover."

Landon summoned courage to his voice. "We don't know the condition of the rover. It's possible it escaped damage."

Doc snuffled and choked. "Wake up, Landon. What do you see? Nothing, yes?"

"We can't see it," he said, "because it's dark, and we didn't leave any lights on inside the rover. Maybe only the floodlights got knocked out."

Ruy staggered to his feet and reached for the rope they had used to climb here. "Then let's go back now. We can still save ourselves."

"There's nothing to go back to," Doc said. "Those rocks crushed the rover."

"Maybe," Ruy said, gasping, "maybe we can walk back to base."

Silence descended around them. The only sounds were the rapid breaths of desperation. Landon knew that they all knew that they wouldn't make it before their air ran out.

Ruy went on. "We could retrieve some extra canisters of oxygen from the rover. They would give us enough time to walk back to base. We can still use the emergency cryo-tanks there, but we have to hurry. Let's go."

"No," Landon said. "I have a better idea. The components for the remote terminal of my tachcom were buried along with Inez in that instability. If I can find them, I can use them to send a message to us in our past, warning us against coming here. Tachyons are really just a form of time travel, see?"

He shivered, remembering the first emission they'd received on Earth before this mission started. It had contained a message they'd decoded as "don't come." Had it come from Landon himself?

"That's not a better idea," Ruy said. His breath came in shallow pants. "That's crazy."

His crewmates knew about tachyons. Why weren't they seeing it? Landon explained again. "It's because they're subatomic particles that travel faster than light. With my equipment, I can use them to travel through time, to warn us before we ever arrive here."

"You mean," said Doc, "our past selves would receive a message from us, here in the present? Has that ever been done before?"

"It's theoretically possible," Landon said. "Van Pelt was working on such a theory before he died."

"But what would happen to *us*," Ruy said, "assuming our past selves heed the warning?"

"As I see it," Landon said, "we don't have many alternatives."

"We'll have a better chance in the cryo-tank."

"Assuming we can get there without dying first," said Doc. "As senior officer, I say we go with the tachyon plan. Lead the way, Dr. Walker."

Landon turned away and headed off before Ruy could complain again. He knew the route by now, trekking across the ridges of the sphinx's hair, crossing to the cheek. Their helmet spotlights showed the terrain where they stepped. The swells and dips indicated that they closed in on the mouth canyon, the site of the disturbance. It had produced an alien hand and had taken Inez, and now that they were returning to the scene, Landon felt anticipation swell within himself. This was also where Chico would've come, looking for the rest of them.

Finally, they reached the wind-swept canyon of the sphinx's mouth. All three of them shone their headlamps throughout the area. There was no evidence of Chico's crashed skimmer. No bootprints from their earlier work. None of the holes remained from their previous excavations. No disturbances indicated they'd ever touched this place. All of it had been smoothed over by the dust storm, including the tools Landon had left behind.

"Shit," said Doc, standing beside Landon.

"We can't dig without our tools," Ruy said. "We should've found a way to bring them back with us."

"It was hard enough to climb up that rope," Doc said.

"Mine are still here somewhere," Landon said with a grunt. "We can hunt around for them with rocks."

Ruy whimpered. "But that's not going to do any good. We couldn't accomplish anything before, not even when we had proper tools. How can we possibly do anything by hand?"

Landon slid down into the crevasse and beckoned for the others to follow. Ruy grumbled and Doc scolded, but they followed him, and they all set to work, clawing with their gloved hands at the fresh deposits of sandy soil.

Landon fought light-headedness as they worked. From fatigue, he decided, calculating how many hours it had been since he'd slept. Not counting cryo-sleep. He felt as if time distorted around them.

At some point he became aware of displaced sounds. Whispers. At first he tried to ignore them, but then goosebumps made the hair on his arms tickle him under his spacesuit liner. Was it the wind starting up again? He saw no puffs of dust, and his suit protected him from the touch of wind, and yet...

It was like...water gurgling.

Then something howled. He jerked backwards from his crouch. What he'd heard had to be the wind. Not water.

But the wind had died. The storm was over.

The howl sounded like an animal yipping. Reminding him of a coyote caught in a trap.

As he was caught.

The howl came again, rolling up out of the stars in the regolith. Then it faded, and he heard again the gurgling sound that running water made. But that was impossible. Even if water existed in the permafrost, he wouldn't hear it flowing like a babbling brook. Anyway, water couldn't exist on a dead world.

Yet, he'd heard running water. Of that, he was certain. Maybe the sounds were coming to him by way of the various pieces of gear he'd lost here—the supraluminal particle sensor, and his tachcom parts.

Ruy cried out beside him. "I've struck something."

Doc aimed her headlamp on Ruy's hole, dispelling the shadows of night.

"How far down?" Landon asked, alert now, scrambling closer.

"About a meter."

The two of them scooped feverishly together, raising dust in a cloud around them. As Landon worked, he felt a tightness grip his chest. He crept backwards, leaning on his haunches and gasping for breath.

Sweat ran down his cheeks. His suit's ventilation system thrummed at a higher level of intensity. Feeling dizzy, he saw Doc's mouth moving through the faceplate—she was talking at him, but he no longer heard her voice.

No. There *was* a voice. Odd, that it wasn't in sync with Doc's lips. It was a husky voice, a slurred voice. Not Doc's. He crawled to the edge of the hole he'd dug near Ruy's.

The voice rose from the depths of the sphinx and sang in his head, made him dizzy. A song...no, a lament. Sobs, joined by others.

"Ti...ti...tri..." they seemed to whisper. It was the wind.

"Tititri..." the wind repeated in a woman's husky voice.

Landon lost his balance as he realized, looking around, that the air was still. There was no wind. Yet, a puff of dust stirred at the bottom of the hole, and a fractured light sparkled from within. A reflection from his headlamp, but...why did it...glitter?

"Doc?" he gasped. But he knew with a mixture of elation and dread that what he'd heard was not Doc's voice.

"Landon," the husky voice whispered again, sounding like the wind. Memory tickled the back of his head. He'd heard that voice before. In the Tititri spaceship. Wrecked, under a glacier in Patagonia.

That voice had been waiting for him when he'd penetrated the alien artifact.

This voice had somehow been activated by the sparkles within the hole that he'd dug. It was coming from within his head, which meant that the voice had gained access to the transmitter in his helmet. It was the voice of the hacker who must have sabotaged communications, aided by the dust storm. So far, the only other link that he'd successfully restored was with the *Centaurus*. Did that mean the hacker's voice was coming from there? From the orbiting ship?

Ruy and Doc must have heard her voice, too, given the way Ruy jerked to attention and Doc dropped to her knees beside Landon.

"I hear a baby crying!" Doc said, clawing at the ground.

"No, what you hear is Commander Masambwa." Ruy tapped the side of his helmet. "Hush. She is trying to tell us what we should do."

They were both wrong. It was Molly! Or rather, it was the alien being who controlled his daughter. She called herself the Titinha, and she lived within Molly, who was now awake and plunging toward rendezvous with a star.

Landon felt frozen in place. His muscles tensed, and his mind screamed at him to leap away from the alien's hold over him. As if that would help. But it didn't matter, because he couldn't move. He couldn't pull himself out of the Titinha's grip.

"There is another way," she whispered, "but you must hurry."

"Hurry, Landon!" Doc cried. "We have to save the baby!"

The Titinha continued to whisper in his ear. "You must find us. As you found us before."

Ruy slapped the side of his helmet and shouted into his close-range mic. "The commander is telling us that they're too close! They cannot brake in time. The star...Proxima..."

"Hurry," said the Titinha, "before—"

"Hello?" Ruy said. "Commander? Come in, please."

The Titinha's voice died in Landon's ears. And he knew with the weight of the universe, that along with her voice dying, so did Molly.

Chapter Eight

Chico no longer felt his arm, crushed against the interior of the skimmer. But pain still overwhelmed him, like tiny bursts of electric shocks pulsing through his head... All the while, Inez chirped at someone behind her. Inez. It had taken *him* to find her. He wanted to snicker, thinking of the incompetent scientist civilians, but it hurt too much.

Captain Inez. *Really?* She wasn't dressed in her standard-issue jumpsuit but wrapped instead in some flowing, shimmering cape, thin as onionskin. It melded to her body and rippled and tinkled as she moved. What the hell? Where in hell was he?

He wondered for a moment about Doc's endorphin theory, producing hallucinations in a post-cryonic state. Maybe that explained this. Was he hallucinating?

Inez moved aside, and a swarm of chirping children surrounded the crumpled skimmer. But they were no kids like he'd ever seen before. They pulled open the door as if it wasn't jammed at all.

And then his ruined arm seared to life with new feeling, blazing with a supernova of fresh pain as the kids slid him out of his cocoon and rolled him onto a homemade litter of cheap canvas, and all of it tied together with dried reeds. Inez stepped close to his side, placed her hands on his helmet, and twisted it off.

"No!" he roared on his last gasp of breath, and pain exploded in a suffocating fog. He was dead for sure without his—

Free. He smelled the sea. Coming from the wind farms of the Colorado desert, he'd always been drawn to great bodies of water. He was like a dowser with a forked stick near an underground spring of water. He could sniff out the scent of saltwater blindfolded.

He inhaled the tangy air, heavy with the vapors of sea foam, and he still lived. Or, if this was what it was like to be dead, then he could handle it.

It couldn't be death. It hurt too much. They jounced him along atop his litter, rolling back and forth from one stick edge to the other. No effing idea if the reeds would hold him in more or less place. He couldn't even curse, not in the presence of kids. His teeth clattered as they carried him with their tiny, bouncing, up-and-down, jarring steps, moving him out of the deep shadows into the white-hot light of day. His eyes felt like they were on fire. He tried to turn his head away from the fire, but his neck wouldn't move. He blinked furiously to force his tired lids open. His eyes puddled with tears, and his vision blurred, but it was all too bright to focus on anything, anyway. He'd never realized before how white-hot the blue-white sky could be. The litter swayed, tipping him finally into welcome shade, cast by a narrow roof that thankfully blanked out the blazing sky.

Flat on his back, he could see that the roof wasn't really a roof. It was the underside of a wide beam, held up at each corner by what looked like bamboo poles. Scaffolding. The kids were carrying him, layer by layer, through scaffolding.

It dawned on him that they weren't kids. And they weren't human.

Pain pressed through him, and he finally allowed his eyelids to sag closed.

2

Chico awoke to cool light and muted air. The soft, rhythmic sound of waves, lapping against the side of whatever building housed him, cooled the fire of his pain. He smelled damp stone. Chirping, twittering music sang in his head.

And then he remembered.

His eyes popped open.

Inez smiled at him and held his hand.

He tried to twist his hand free, but some sort of vise held him. Maybe it was a cast. A sling tangled him into a web that bound him to a rounded, form fitting, half-shell of a bed.

"Comfy?" Inez said, patting his hand and letting go. As she withdrew her hand, glittering pin drops woven within the fabric of her sleeve clinked softly. Then a web came out of nowhere to press against his released flesh.

He was a prisoner.

In some sort of room with a gray stone wall and a stone ceiling that looked too low. It barely skimmed Inez's head, and she wasn't exactly a tall woman. Behind her, high in the wall, an open slit gave him a slice of the view outside—sparkling blue water, a rim of distant, hazy mountain peaks, and a blue sky.

"Where...am I?" His voice croaked, but it worked.

"My best estimate," Inez said in a pleasant voice, as if she reported the weather, "after what I've learned these past ten years that I have been living here with them, is that you and I are approximately three and a half billion years into our past."

149

He choked on his spit. "And this is...the same planet?"

"The riddle of the sphinx is that it protects a portal to the past. A gateway through time."

"So that's where I landed? That thing back there that I slammed into was the *sphinx*?"

She nodded and blinked.

He thought about it for half a second and then said, "Naw. That ain't Proxima up there in the sky. Proxima's not that bright."

"Apparently, from our perspective now, it's a star like our sun, but it's starting to lose mass—"

"Can't happen." He snorted, and then regretted the resulting stab of fire through his head.

She went on, ignoring his protests. "Until finally, Proxima will become the red dwarf that you and I recognize when we are born more than three billion years into this future."

"It doesn't happen that way. But never mind. Let's say you're right. Then all we have to do to go home again is go back through the time portal."

She sighed. "I am afraid not. It seems to only work one way. *Most* of the time. Some have tried it. For instance, the hand we saw. It didn't work then."

"How do we make it work for us?" He couldn't believe he was having this conversation. Or that the captain was accepting her screwball reality so placidly. Then again, she believed in the luck of her *figa*, which still dangled from its chain round her throat.

"We can't."

It was as if she'd resigned herself to being stuck here—three *billion* years in the past? He didn't think so.

"There must be a way. We'll find it. Maybe the kids will tell us."

"They're not kids," she said. "They're Tititri. And they're adults. They have no child phase in their life cycle outside of the egg."

His brains swam inside his head. She was sounding like Doc, and he couldn't figure it out, except for his need to get the hell out of here. Straining, he lifted his head from the cradle-like bed and pressed against the silky fibers of the web, criss-crossing across him, stretching from one side of the cradle to the other.

They didn't break.

"Help me out of here, will you?" He had to get back home. Stuff to do. Babes to impress. He struggled harder. The fibers of the web didn't stretch far enough apart for escape.

"Relax," Inez said, slipping her hand through one of the holes of the webbing to pat him. "Your egg is healing you. Let it work."

"*My* egg?" He didn't like the sound of that. Something tickled deep inside. "Who designed this thing?"

She smiled. "The Tititri. We have to help them. They need us."

3

"Commander?" Ruy shouted. "I can't hear you!"

Landon felt as if the core of his entire being folded up and withered away, disintegrating to dust. As the alien's hand and arm had done.

Ruy's glove tapped the side of his helmet as he sobbed. "I...I

151

lost her. The link. It's...gone! They're gone. The *Centaurus*! The ship must've gone too close to Proxima and got pulled in."

Landon's knees gave out beneath him, but he caught himself in time before crumpling to the ground.

Ruy went on, mercilessly. "It would've incinerated instantly, if it even took that long."

Quivers rolled through Landon, and racking sobs overcame him.

"Shut up, already!" Doc's shout, directed at Ruy, rang in Landon's head. Then her arms encircled Landon. Even through their spacesuits he could feel the comforting pulse of her nearness.

He couldn't believe... His baby girl... Gone...

Then he remembered.

Zyvors.

The Tititris' enemies.

Who else could've orchestrated everything so neatly? The Zyvors must've controlled the anomaly, which had pulled the *Centaurus* off course, requiring more fuel. It was as if they'd flung the ship into a star to get rid of their enemies once and for all.

Molly, the innocent bystander. A casualty, in the name of the Zyvors.

Loathing spread through him, poisoning his soul. He wished he'd paid closer attention to the Titinha when he'd come face to face with her under the glacier in Patagonia. He wished he'd heard more of the little information that she'd given him about her culture's long-term enemies.

"Landon, Landon," Doc crooned, "everything will be okay, yes?"

The *Centaurus*... Gone... None of them could get home.

What was the use?

Unless...

He could undo it. This disaster, and all the rest. He had to see his plan through.

If only he had more time.

The Titinha had told him just now that there was another way. Could he find it? He needed his tachcom, so that he could send a message back through time, a message that would prevent the disaster of this entire mission from ever happening. If he sent that message, maybe he would wake up in his own bed back at ISA headquarters in Goiás. Or maybe even farther back in time than that—back to his days on SpaceHab. Back to his days with Summer, before everything went wrong.

If he could find their way through time, they wouldn't need a spaceship for travel.

"Look!" Ruy gasped and lurched backwards.

Pebbles rattled. Sand and dusty soil slid around Landon's knees, snake-like, as if alive, swirling between the fresh holes they'd dug. Doc pulled him back as the holes widened and merged. Sparkles of light opened up the bottom. Steps led down into a tunnel.

"Up there!" Ruy shouted somewhere behind Landon. "What's that?"

Landon tore his gaze away from the tunnel's opening to turn around and look up into the night sky, where Ruy pointed. A light beam sliced the sky and plunged into the tunnel, highlighting the steps with violet light.

"It's the anomaly," Ruy said in a slow but shaky voice. "It's got to be the same gateway that took the captain away. And

Chico, too. That would explain why we cannot find any trace of them."

"But where did it take them?" Doc said.

Ruy shrugged. "Another place. Another universe. It was an open gateway to another world, and then it closed. Now it is open again."

"In that case," Landon said, creeping closer to the tunnel's entrance, "let's not waste anymore time." He squatted to lower himself into the tunnel.

"Where do you think you are you going?" Doc said with a shriek.

"Down there."

"But it's not safe!"

"Does it matter?" It was their last chance. *His* last chance to find his equipment that could send the message to the past to undo all of this. Landon's boot scraped against something solid below him.

He ducked his head to ease under the sloping ceiling, but the narrow foothold gave way just then. His feet slid out from beneath him, and he fell, dropping away from the purple light that had illuminated the entrance. His arms flung up, fingered gloves groping, clawing. Nothing connected, and he slid farther. His helmet light winked out, and he saw nothing.

"Landon!"

Pebbles rattled against him as he scraped down the dark incline. He hoped his suit could withstand this rattling abuse.

Then the soles of his outstretched boots rammed against a ledge, and he bent his legs, absorbing the shock. He reached out with his arms to brace himself for the rebound, and he caught something that felt like a notch in the wall. It slipped from his grasp, and he flipped sideways, landing on his butt. No purple light embraced him. There was only the dark.

4

Chico didn't know how long he lay in the web-encased cradle Inez had called an egg, listening to the rhythmic swishing of the sea. Ten years for her, at least, or so she'd said. Long enough for her to make sense out of the chirping sounds the Tititri keepers made.

He was no linguist like her, but he had to admit that even he was beginning to sense meaning, just from the tone and pattern of their chirps when the kids came into his room to poke at him through his web. But Inez, hell, she seemed to be carrying on long conversations with them. After a few twerps and tweets she translated stuff that had to be far more extensive than just the few twittering sounds he'd heard. It was as if they communicated on a telepathic level, once they got past the barrier of chirps.

He figured that once he returned home, he'd be the hero of the century for bringing back news of alien first contact.

It almost made up for his disappointment, losing out on the battle he'd anticipated waging against angry aliens. These keeper kids, he had to admit, were just too damned friendly. He called them kids, but they clearly weren't.

And one of them was downright...

He hesitated over using one of his favorite all-time words: "sexy." He was no pervert, but damn. She looked like a babe, with all the necessary human parts in the right places, shrunk down and attached to the frame the size of—

No. They were no kids, and especially not this one. She sounded like a songbird, and she examined him with the precision of a scientist's touch. He had to remember what she really was, and remembering doused the flames of any rising thoughts. She was an *alien*. Hell, for all he knew, maybe she wasn't even a "she." He wasn't that desperate. Not yet.

He might've lain here in his half-shell for weeks, just he and his thoughts. Or it might've been hours. Time was a concept that he could not track. He hadn't even experienced the urges of daily bodily functions. Either the egg took care of that for him, in ways he couldn't imagine, or else time was suspended.

If not for listening to the chirps and twitters, he might've thought that *he* was suspended. In a state of cognitive awareness.

But eventually the cradle finished healing him, and eventually his keepers withdrew the webbing. The air filled with music as he rolled up to the rim of his egg and over the top. His damaged arm functioned with only the slightest tweaks of pain. Inez, rustling in her onionskin cape, caught him on the other side and propped him up onto his feet. He didn't really need any assistance. He felt brand-new, not stiff and sluggish as he would've expected, after having lain flat on his ass for an indeterminate amount of time. The stone room echoed with approving chirps.

"They are pleased," Inez said, nodding at his keepers. He and Inez towered over them. He had to admit, she was right. They were no kids. "They have never grown an alien before."

A chill tickled through him. "You mean 'healed'."

"No, I mean 'grow'."

He shrugged, and it didn't hurt. Inez always was one for semantics. "My body heals itself with enough time. Anyway, why did they want to help me?"

"I will show you. Shall we take a walk?"

Inez led him through a maze of stone corridors, and a procession of the twittering, kid-like Tititri followed. He had to duck his head in a few places, where the ceilings were too low for him. He felt a swell of pleasure, having measured the shortest from his class at the Academy. Size had always rubbed him raw. He'd turned it around into his advantage back then, becoming the fastest of his class. Now, he could finally relax. He had nothing to prove anymore.

Light blazed from the end of the damp corridor, and Inez pulled him to a stop. She took an empty bowl from one of their keepers, turned it upside down, and then placed it over his head, helmet style. Goggles extended down, covering his eyes with special lenses that filtered the light pouring in from the outside and toned down the light's intensity. He blinked, and they continued outward, helmet bobbing loosely atop the crown of his head. She, apparently, had adapted enough that she didn't need any protection against the light.

They stood on a narrow shoreline, squeezed below a city of stone buildings that overlooked the sea he'd heard from his cradle. Or maybe it was a vast lake. He couldn't tell, because mountain peaks rose from the horizon on the far side of the sea. Although he tasted salt in the air, and considering the rolling size of the waves, halfway to his knees, he assumed this body of water was larger than a lake. He saw no disturbance out there in the water to cause the waves, other than a steady wind on his cheeks, carrying the taste of salt.

"They tell me this is the last body of water on Titra," Inez said, "which is what they call this world. This is all that's left of their oceans, which used to be fed from the ice melt from their polar caps."

"And that?" He nodded at the sphinx, rising up from the middle of the sea, as if the sole occupant of an island. Scaffolding lined its sides. Still under construction.

"They call it their ark," Inez said, following his gaze.

"Ark? As in Noah and his massive flood?" He saw no hint of rising waters. And she had just told him that water was going away. Not rising. His brain hurt. Except for the sea, the rest of the landscape—what he could see beyond the stone city at the edge of the sea—appeared desert dry. As barren as the plains of home.

Clearly, he wasn't home.

"In a manner of speaking," Inez said with her trademark, tinkling laugh. "It is their massive undertaking in the face of otherwise, certain death. Their star is losing mass, you see."

"That's shit."

She smiled and beckoned with her arm. "C'mon, I'll show you."

She turned away from the sea and led him through cobbled alleys that wound between stone walls, the procession of Tititri keepers in tow. Troops—or should he say flocks?—of their twittering brethren gathered in doorways and watched them pass. Inez, who seemed to have won them over, waved and smiled in greeting. She nodded at him to do the same, but all he could do was grunt.

If this was the same planet he'd landed the shuttlecraft on, he didn't recognize this sloping terrain. She was leading him up the longest, most winding way to the highest hill. By the time they crested its summit, he was gasping for breath, feeling the burn of the thinness of the air in his lungs.

A round, stone building with a domed roof sat atop the hill. The pillars of its structure were stone slabs, and he startled at their sight. He'd seen them before. They were the components of the semicircle of rock soldiers. He'd put the shuttlecraft down close to them. Over there—his head twisted to his left—he'd erected the twin bubbles of base. But this—he turned back to the right—*this* was what those remaining slabs of rock soldiers had looked like before they'd fallen apart into ruins. Hell. With that domed roof, it almost looked like—

"This is their observatory," Inez said. "The Tititri are quite advanced with their astronomical observations. Not only have they studied the three stars of their own solar system, but they know all about ours. They know how promising Earth looks as a new home for them, once this planet becomes too inhospitable. As we know it will."

"Why go so far from home, when they have their own sister planet next door?"

"Right now, it's a seared rock." She grinned. "It won't inhabit the goldilocks zone for another three and a half billion years."

"Okay, there's another tiny problem. What about *us*?"

"They don't want to interfere with us."

"And you believe that?" Something didn't sit right with him. Something was making his skin crawl.

She smiled again. "Sure, and you will, too, once you see—"

"Look," he said, trying to explain, "they sound like birds, but they don't fly like birds. If they think they're going to use that sphinx for space flight, they're crazier than I thought. They're not going to get very far. Not even I could make it fly."

She laughed, and her goddamned cheer was beginning to annoy him. "Of course the ark won't fly. They have already sent probes to remotely study the developing life on Earth."

From the top of the hill, he could just see the sphinx's head rise above the horizon line. "There must be another planet closer to them, one in their own system, one that's not a seared rock. Why go all the way to Earth?"

"You'll see, if you'd only have some patience." She pointed up to the sky. "Did you notice how much brighter their sun seems to ours?"

"It's kind of hard to miss." He shrugged, and his helmet slid atop his ears. "I'm no physicist like Brandt, but I don't think it would look brighter if it's losing mass, like you said."

"It looks that bright because there are devices installed around Proxima that intensify the process of stripping atmosphere from its planets. Those same devices shield the work of the Zyvors, as they siphon off mass from multiple star systems."

"The...*what*?"

"The Zyvors. It means 'star-eaters' in the Tititri language. They are the mortal enemies, not only of the Tititri but also of any civilizations that dwell within multiple star systems. Star-eaters feed off the power of such systems, amassing the mass they collect in the galactic center. The Tititri believe it's the Zyvor effort to ward off encroaching galaxies. Star-eaters don't care who is destroyed in the process. This makes Earth look even more promising to the Tititri, who believe they will be safe from the star-eaters in a single star system such as ours."

The half-helmet suddenly felt extra heavy, and he staggered on his feet. Even if he made it home, what would home be like, overrun by aliens?

5

Silence fell around Landon, deep inside the sphinx. He'd fallen through the dark passageway tunneling from the mouth of the beast down its esophagus and into its belly. He flicked on his helmet light—murmuring thanks that it still worked—and cast its thin, narrow beam around him. All he saw was rising dust, drifting like motes into cloud shapes. No tachcom parts. His throat constricted, and he twisted around to peer back up the tunnel he'd so ungracefully slid down.

"Landon!" Doc gasped in his earpiece, as if she stood beside him instead of above him, out there, on top of the sphinx. "I'm coming, too!"

The loose rock on the slope leading up to the surface shifted. Pebbles slid down on him in a rattling rain. Then her dark shape appeared in the shadows above his head and scraped down the slope toward him, catching on a ledge.

He grabbed her boot and eased her down. Her arms flapped around her, then snagged around Landon. They stood there together, clasping each other, rocking together. Then Doc broke away and looked around herself.

"What is this place?"

"We're caught on some sort of platform."

"No, I mean the steps. Someone...built them, yes?"

"The Tititri." It was obvious. "What about Ruy?"

"He's staying above. Someone has to string down a cable to fish out your equipment. Us, too." She shone her helmet light on the sloping walls of the tunnel, bouncing it along stair-step protrusions from each rock. "What is this place?"

"Steps, going down into the sphinx," Landon said.

"But *why*?"

"Someone used this place."

"The Tititri, you think?"

He nodded. Even now, someone used it. Maybe the Zyvors. He hoped so, because he would catch up to them. And then he would pound those sons of bitches to pulp.

Their heavy breathing rasped in his ears. He even thought he heard his heart as well. Pounding, hammering, echoing against the stone walls that...someone—aliens—had built. A passage...to where? What was it used for?

"Look." Doc aimed her helmet light ahead, onto the opposite wall of the tunnel, beyond the ledge where they stood in relative safety. "What do you see?" Her light bobbed on the walls, reflecting the excitement in her voice.

"Hold it still. Is that a design of some sort?"

"More than that. Look again." She reached across to the wall of carefully fitted blocks. Her gloved fingers traced the rock, outlining designs. "It's a carving," she whispered.

He sucked in his breath, recognizing the triangles within larger triangles. "It's like what I saw on the alien's arm."

They stood in reverent silence, staring back and forth at the decorated wall.

"Maybe that alien took your tachcom parts," Doc said.

"Let's go find out." Landon stepped around Doc and headed into the darkness beyond his helmet light. "If they're down here, I'll find them."

He bounded down the narrow steps, which led him lower and lower into the maw of the sphinx. He swung his head back and forth, searching with his helmet light for his lost equipment,

162

finding instead the carvings of triangles. Maybe the design represented gateways within gateways.

Loose rock littered the steps and slid beneath his boots. He stumbled downward, and Doc clattered behind him. Angling down into darkness, the tunnel curved first to the right, then to the left. They stepped carefully, groping the sides of the stone blocks, climbing over occasional rubble. His gloved hands slid along the walls that the Tititri had touched, and he felt their presence. They'd invaded his life, and he would see this through to the end.

"When I assemble my tachcom," he said, pausing, "and send a message of warning to us in the past, I hope like hell we listen. Otherwise, all this—it's for nothing."

"*Non.* It's not for nothing." Doc pushed past him, looking back over her shoulder at him.

"Hey, be careful! Watch where you're going!"

She didn't listen to him. "*Shit!*"

Rocks tumbled, crashing against a distant surface, bounding and rebounding. At the edge of Landon's beam of light, he saw her fall, dipping out of his sight, along with the fading sound of her scream. He heard a thud, then more scraping, and finally, the last thud.

"Doc!" He sprang after her, jumping down two block-steps at a time, carefully, so that he didn't fall into whatever trap she hadn't seen. Farther down, he stood on another ledge, staring into a pit of darkness. The light from his helmet couldn't penetrate far enough to reveal the bottom. Her own light had winked out.

"Renee!" he called, using Doc's real name.

The only sound that answered him, however, was the

scattering of rocks. He stood at the edge of a gaping hole, where a section of the tunnel's steps had caved in. "Doc!" he called again. "Can you hear me?"

He was already moving toward one wall, where he groped for a foothold at the edge of the pit. His boot kicked loose a rock, which tumbled away, and he visualized it falling on her, penetrating a seal, or her helmet. He leaned against a rocky protrusion in the wall and held his breath. His feet slipped, and more pebbles rattled down the sides of these broken steps and bounced against the floor of the pit below.

"Renee, dammit!"

Carefully, his boot tested the cave-in until he found another solid block below, extending from the side of the pit. He lowered himself onto it, and when it held, he released his grip from above and crouched down to repeat this process. A whimper interrupted his descent.

His heart and lungs felt as if they would explode in his chest. "Why the hell didn't you look where you were going?"

"Good to hear the sound of your pleasant voice, Landon," she said with an unconvincing laugh.

Trembling, he kicked loose another rock, which tumbled away.

"Hey, watch it!" she shouted.

"Can you move?"

"Yes, I... Shit! No, I think my leg is broken."

"Keep still, then. I'll be there in a minute. Does your light work?"

"*Non.*"

"Okay, then. Just hang on."

Slowly, he crept down the jagged sides of the pit. Finally,

his helmet light swept across the bottom. He scrambled across rubble, and a few steps farther on, he found her. One leg bent at an unnatural angle.

Hurrying to her side, he reached for her suitpac and checked her stats. No broken seals. He breathed a sigh of relief. Her vitals appeared normal, too. He cradled her gently. "It's all right," he whispered, hoping this was so. "You have your beltpac?"

"Of course." She tried to lift herself onto her elbows but stopped with a cry.

He unzipped the pac from her waist and sat down on the next step to open it.

"What is your plan now?"

"Give you something for your pain, then keep going. I'll find my equipment and send that message. Then, hopefully, we'll vanish right out of here, reappearing back in time. That should fix your leg, too."

"Let's hope it works, yes? Give me that pac. I can take care of myself. You go on, go look for your tachcom, if you are so brave."

"With pleasure." As he stood to thrust the pac at her, his light played on the walls at the bottom of this pit. A passage narrowed ahead into the shape of a small triangle.

"What's that?" he whispered.

She strained to lift herself enough to see. "Looks like the end of the tunnel."

"Wait here."

"Where could I possibly go?"

"I'll be right back," he said, following his beam of light along the narrowing tunnel. Dust rose before him in waving fingers.

Damned dust!

Groping through the cloud, he continued toward a small, black triangle—the end of the tunnel? A gateway within a gateway. Could his equipment have fallen this far?

The walls of the tunnel funneled to a triangular hole, littered with a pile of broken blocks. Ducking, he crawled through the small, open gate. His helmet beam drifted through blackness, failing to locate anything within reach to illuminate.

"It's a cavern," he managed to say, even though he felt as if someone—something—had knocked the wind out of him. He was in an underground, artificial world, one that he couldn't see. The city at the end of the stairs? A failed habitat? He stumbled a few steps into it.

"Landon!" Doc screeched. "I changed my mind, and now I order you to come back! If you go in there too far, you will lose your way and never find the entrance to the tunnel again."

He froze. His helmet light swept wide arcs across the floor, level ground, caked with the dust of undisturbed eons. His boots were the first to make prints in countless thousands of years.

Prints. He'd find his way out.

Chapter Nine

Not even Chico could comprehend the level of sophistication of the interior of the Tititri observatory. From the outside, it had appeared downright crude with its round structure of stone. But when he followed Inez inside, hell, it was another matter.

"Fire!" he shouted, tripping over his feet in his haste to retreat. An inferno roiled in the center of the circular building. It looked as if the entire observatory was going up in flames, yet he didn't feel any heat.

Inez laughed at him and beckoned him closer to the fire. "Relax. It's just a 3-D image of Proxima, projected into this viewing well. The scopes of this observatory beam their images here. Think of this as walking inside a giant viewscope."

He shook the tension from his shoulders, smoothed his cowlick, and gave a shaky, snort of a laugh. This wasn't so unusual, not really. It looked something like a hologram pit. Nothing out of his range of experience. He just didn't like being caught unaware, coming face to face with a star, so to speak. When the initial shock faded, he hurried after Inez, who strolled unafraid along the walkway that circumnavigated the perimeter of the tubular well.

"You don't have to look through an eyepiece in this observatory," she said. "Rather, the image comes to you, already

167

filtered for safe viewing. What do you think?"

"Very handy." He wasn't afraid, either.

He'd never stood so close to a star before, even if it was a virtual monster. The star towered above him, as tall and massive as a gyrating wind turbine from home. He reached out his arm to touch it, thinking he could. He felt...nothing. But he was close enough...

A shadowy outline of some sort of a grid traced across the fire. It looked like chain mail trying to encase the rounded edges of a blazing star, trying to hold in its mass, except for the fiery plumes that licked through the looped links.

"What *is* that?" he whispered, in awe.

"I told you already. It's them. The Zyvors. Their devices resemble a net, and they use it to constrict star mass as they prepare to siphon it off. The Tititri believe that the Zyvors steal the mass through wormholes."

"Impossible."

"I wouldn't be so quick to dismiss it. The Tititri are advanced far beyond our understanding. They've already mapped out over a hundred wormholes. Besides, you and I are privileged to know the outcome of their battles. We've seen what Proxima becomes billions of years from now. And right there is the cause." She pointed at the sphere of fire, distorted inside a tubular well that extended multiple levels up into the domed roof overhead. "You can see the Zyvor star net for yourself. Now do you believe me?"

The answer was still no. He was pretty sure he was dreaming all this. He was pretty sure he was dead in another reality.

But he could play along.

He whistled. "What do they want *us* to do? It seems like

they've got it all worked out for themselves, if they plan an exodus to Earth. Why do they even need you and me?"

"They don't. It's Landon. They need Landon."

Shit. Even in death, the famous tachyon man was getting all the glory. Glory that Chico deserved. "Let me guess. He doesn't get the job done, am I right?"

Landon must fail in whatever they wanted him for, because otherwise there would've been aliens all over Earth by the time Chico would be born and grow up on the wind farm of Colorado. He didn't remember ever encountering any aliens in his previous life, still to play out in the distant future. Strange humans, maybe, but no aliens. He would've remembered chirping humanoids.

"We can change the outcome," Inez said, disappearing from sight as the walkway curved around to the backside of the fiery ball.

"You want to make them need us, instead of Landon, to do his job?"

"No, I mean we can bring him here, so that he can fulfill his destiny."

"What you're talking about is rewriting history as we know it." A chill ran through him as he hurried to catch up. "That'd be like fucking with time travel. Maybe we'll never be born. We'll poof out of existence." When he reached the spot where he'd last seen her, she wasn't there. Had she poofed? Panic welled up in his throat, closing off air passages, and he fought his invisible strangler for breath.

"Does that worry you?" Her voice floated through a black wall, and then he spied a narrow rectangle quivering in the wall. It must be a doorway, about chin high, and obscured with a sheet of black, foggy smoke. Holding his breath, he ducked and squeezed through sideways.

Yeah, he was plenty worried. He didn't want to deprive anyone—himself, most of all—of never being born.

"Maybe," she said from the other side of the curtain, "we'll have another purpose. We'll still exist, but maybe we'll inhabit the body of someone else."

He opened his mouth to protest and swallowed some fog. It tasted like... The weed his mother used to smoke.

"That's shit."

When the fog cleared from his face, he saw a giant, blue ball, almost as big as the virtual sphere of Proxima. It was another image, cast inside another tubular well, a walk-in viewscope. Not on fire, it must be a planet.

"What do they need Landon for, anyway?" he asked.

Inez rested one knee against a railing that separated the walkway from the image of the hanging planet. "To save this," she said, sweeping one arm across the vista. "Earth."

He studied the sphere, mostly blue with oceans. "That's not Earth. The continents are wrong."

"The continents haven't shifted yet into the patterns you recognize."

He felt as if the walls were pushing their darkness in on him. His heartbeat fluttered in his chest. His throat tightened, and he sputtered, finding his voice. "Let me guess. They want Landon to save Earth from the Zyvors, right?"

She stood there grinning at him, as if she'd saved him from his crashed skimmer just for her personal amusement of watching him fall apart into a helpless, mewling puddle.

He was getting damned tired of this shit. "Look, let me at

them. I can do it. Besides, Landon isn't here, and we are. What do we need to do?"

"The Titinha will tell us. She's waiting for us at the ark."

He came alert. "She? Is she anything like the keepers who strapped me down in bed?"

"Hardly," Inez said with a laugh. "You can think of her as queen of the Tititri, if that will help you give her the proper respect."

"What do you want me to do? Am I supposed to thank her for her hospitality?"

"Just try not to embarrass me." She grinned, amused again. "Luckily, you don't speak their language yet."

"Right. I never could pass bird talk at the Academy."

He wondered, as Inez led him along the walkway around Earth, was she—the queen who was not really a queen—even a "she"? Was he supposed to accept her as *his* queen? Thank her for "rescuing" him? He wasn't sure how much respect he could show a bird-like kid with human features, but oh well. He wasn't sure how grateful he really felt, if at all.

Inez faded from sight, ducking through another fog curtain in the black wall behind Earth. He held his breath and dove in after her, anticipating the next celestial wonder. What would confront him this time in the next viewing well?

When the fog cleared, he felt the prickle of disappointment. There was no star. No planet suspended in front of him. Instead, he faced a plain, circular chamber, only a few meters in diameter, and it was empty except for the purple fog that swirled across a low, curving rim of what looked like the base of an egg-cradle. It sat in the center of the circular room. He shifted on his feet, impatient to find the observatory's exit and get over to the ark to meet the bird queen.

Inez caught him by the arm. "Careful," she said.

"Hey, there's nothing to break in here."

"Only your neck. You have to position yourself correctly as you enter the transporter. I find it helps to make a *figa* of my fist."

"Huh?"

"Here, I'll show you." Inez held up her hand and slipped her thumb between her first two fingers, making a fist. "It's for good luck."

"My luck ran out a long time ago."

"Fine, then. Have a bumpy ride, if that's what you wish." She grabbed him with her non-*figa* hand and pulled him towards the purple fog. "The Tititri have learned how to harness wormholes for transportation. This one will take us over to the ark. Stop fidgeting, and relax. Here we go."

They stepped over the rim of the low wall.

2

Landon stumbled forward, the bulk of his spacesuit slowing his step. He played his helmet's spot upward, into the dark of the cavernous interior. Nearby, swirling air currents disturbed the beam of light. Shadows surrounded him inside the hollow core of the sphinx's body.

"Landon!" Doc screamed at him over the suit com. "Don't leave me alone here. It's dark without you and your light."

He toggled the volume down and continued. Coughing, he felt as if he were choking on the dust that his boots stirred, even though he knew that was false. He breathed from his suit's oxygen tank. Still...the impossible surrounded him everywhere. *Damned dust.* Dust was to blame for all that had gone wrong on this mission.

Stumbling over litter, stepping lightly in the lowered gravity, he felt almost floating. Until he bumped into a solid object. He rebounded and fell backwards, stirring up more dust. Scrambling to his feet, he groped for the thing that had stopped him. A low wall, about hip height, stood before him. He touched its surface, smoothing its contours with his gloves. An icy coldness penetrated the fabric of his suit, and he jerked his hand away.

Shapes slowly emerged through the thinning dust. Rectangular shapes. Rows and columns of rectangles. He was reminded of one of the old cemeteries on Earth, ostentatiously taking up space, displaying fields and fields of headstones. He forced his frozen body to move, thudding slowly along the perimeter of the wall that had stopped him. It seemed to encircle this field of headstones. Fresh swirls of disturbed dust rose to obscure the objects—headstones?—on the other side of the wall.

He finally came to a break in the wall, littered with loose rubble, and he paused there, waiting for the dust to clear. He played his light on the shapes. Rectangular shapes. Closer now, he could see that they were oblong pedestals, with irregular outlines on top. Hundreds of them lined up in rows, fading into the shadows beyond the range of his light. Countless more lay even farther away.

He stepped through the opening in the wall and aimed his light on the surface contours of the nearest pedestal. In the instant before a curtain of dust obscured the shape, he thought he recognized the outline of a prone body.

He staggered backwards. Blinking didn't help clear his vision. It didn't change what he thought he'd seen.

He stepped forward again and reached out through the dust, his hand hovering above the irregular shape. Slowly, slowly, he lowered his fingers to touch the thing's outline. Even through his gloves it felt like an arm...a shoulder...breasts... His hand jerked back. A stone statue, a *humanoid* statue of someone in repose.

He thought of the rock he'd found. Ruy had said it was a petrified bone. Had it come from this place?

Then, these weren't...statues.

They were petrified *humanoids*.

There must be hundreds of them. Hundreds more, beyond the shadows. Thousands, altogether. He wandered, dazed, along the rows, stirring up more dust.

He continued on, into the heart of this place. Far above, on the surface of the planet, the sphinx had stared for eons up to the heavens, as if waiting for the *Centaurus* to arrive. Now it was gone. Pulled into the fires of Proxima. He shuddered, suppressing the urge to throw up.

He chin bumped his voice link louder. "They're petrified, Renee," he said, as if the doc stood right here beside him, able to see the sorry remains of the Tititri civilization.

"Landon, come out of there," she said.

"They're like the bone we found. Only these people were petrified with their flesh still intact."

"You've found...people?"

"Hundreds and hundreds of them."

"Petrified...people?"

"Petrified aliens. They are the Tititri who were signaling us

174

tachyonically. They wanted our help, but we were too late."

"Help for what?"

"What else? To save them from whatever resulted in their petrifaction."

"Landon," she said with an explosive sigh, "you've been in there long enough. It's time for us to go back."

"Not yet." What good was it, to go back, without a spaceship to take them home? Their only hope was for him to find his tachcom. He moved along the rows, faster now, almost skipping.

"Why would any race petrify itself?" Doc said over his link.

"Don't know. Must've been desperate. They intended to do it. Look at this place. They built it to store themselves in it. That's the riddle of their sphinx."

What was he supposed to do? Restore them, somehow?

Ahead, through the dust, he saw a circle of pedestals, raised on a dais, apart from the rest of the petrified Tititri. A small instrument sat atop the central pedestal, and he gasped when he recognized its boxy shape. *His* supraluminal particle sensor. Silent now.

3

Chico had never fallen through a wormhole before. Pilot's school at the Academy hadn't covered the subject.

Resisting Inez's advice to relax, he tensed his muscles as he stepped with her over the low rim and into the half-shell that she'd called a transporter. It felt as if invisible arms wrapped around him, encircling him. Then the floor fell out from beneath his feet. Unseen forces whipped him round and round, smearing his skin with the sensation of lubricated rubber. It was a condom, the size of a body wrap. The forces wrestled him through their funhouse, making him relive his personal demons of uncontrolled flying.

He'd watched a tornado pick up a barn once and carry it away, shredding it board by board, and that's how he felt now. Suspended, squeezed, and shredded.

Shit. Maybe he should've listened. He still didn't believe the *figa* would make this ride any easier, but evidently she did. Anyway, it was too late to twist his fingers now. He couldn't make any of his body parts move.

As suddenly as it had started, it was over. His feet touched solid ground, although his head continued to spin. He had to wonder how practical was this means of travel. It would've been easier to take a boat across to the island sphinx, wouldn't it? But the Tititri had apparently wanted to show off their power.

Don't fuck with us, he imagined their twittering chirps to mean.

"Wheee," said Inez beside him, as if she'd just stepped off a 3-g coaster in a thrill park. She took a tipsy step forward, out of the purple cloud that swirled at their feet, and up onto a sloping walkway. "Here we are, inside the ark."

He looked around, but he wasn't impressed. Had he and Inez even traveled anywhere? It was hard to tell through the dim murk. Here looked the same as the darkened interior of the observatory, with its circular room behind the image of Earth. But then, as he followed her along the narrow platform that led up from the purple cloud, he detected a slight musty smell.

Gone was the parched dust taste in the observatory's air.

Here, water had seeped inside.

The walkway spiraled up, protruding from the edge of

circular walls. Below his feet, the purple cloud frothed. Above his head, a square of golden light glowed in the dark, beckoning to him like an exit light. This way out.

Mama used to always keep a light burning at night when he'd been out, enjoying other types of funhouses.

Longing filled him. He wanted to go home. He was tired of this shit.

He caught up to Inez and tugged on her sleeve. "How are we...going to get home?"

He *had* to get home. His mother would die if he didn't, and he wasn't going to be responsible for that. He'd done enough damage already to her blood pressure. Enough was enough. It was time to get the hell out of here. Cut his losses and go home, tail between his legs, if he had to.

"If we help her," Inez said, "the Titinha will help us."

"Look, maybe she could just tell me how to manipulate that cloud down there. Then I can do the rest."

"Fair enough."

He pushed past her and marched onward to the square of golden light.

"Chico, wait...," she said, gasping behind him.

He burst out of the shaft containing the purple cloud and into a cavern flooded with light. The impact of light blinded him, and he staggered, slowing his step while his eyes watered. Inez caught up to him from behind, and two figures emerged from the bright blur ahead.

They chirped back and forth as Chico's vision slowly adjusted. He couldn't see the source of the light, but light blazed everywhere. A spacious room soared around him in the shape of a sphere. He was standing in the belly of a giant egg, which he figured was as large as a hangar that could store a dozen or more full-sized shuttlecrafts. Except, this hangar housed hundreds of egg cradles. Thousands, maybe. Racks containing more of the things stacked above his head, and all of them looked empty.

"What is this place?" he said. "A manufacturing center for egg cradles?"

But Inez wasn't listening to him. She was busy communicating with the kids. If they were meant to be guards, then Chico figured he could easily overpower them if necessary. The tops of their heads barely reached his chin, and they didn't appear to carry weapons. Naked from the waist up—they were males—their torsos were covered with tattoos of triangular designs.

"We have to wait," Inez said.

Sure. What was the rush of Queenie calling them here, only to make them wait? He bet he knew why. "Another little demonstration of the power of Queen Titinha?"

"Titinha is not her name; it's her title."

"Okay, so she's not a queen."

"Not as you understand. She occupies the number one caregiver position of the Tititri. She was grown for this position."

"Grown?"

"In her egg."

"Right."

"She controls the transporter, keeping it open, but she requires our help. She needs yours specifically, since you are an expert pilot."

"What does she want to know? How to survive a crash?"

Inez laughed. "Trust me, the Titinha already knows far more about survival than you could ever hope to know. This ark is proof. She is the supreme being, and as such, she is the keeper of the Tititri throughout time. She is the single individual who embodies all collective understanding of past, present, and future."

He whistled. "Wow. That's a lot of eggs in one basket." He couldn't help himself. "What happens if she falls and breaks her ankle?"

Inez tipped her head sideways at him. "Her egg would heal her, as yours healed you."

"Everyone has their own egg, custom built for them? How'd they know how to build one for *me*, an alien?"

"They took your genetic reading, of course."

Of course. "It still seems kind of risky. And, anyway, time is just a concept. How do you put all of time into one being?"

"I have already told you that they are advanced far beyond our understanding."

"Don't give me that bullshit. What happens if she's...let's say, permanently incapacitated? All Tititri knowledge dies with her?"

"Essentially, her egg would make another copy of her."

"Damn. I've got to get me one of those things."

"She will tell you more about it herself."

Finally, the kid-like guards ushered them across the showroom floor displaying egg cradles and over to the far wall, covered with triangular carvings. The guard pressed against one of the triangles, and the blocks in the wall shifted, revealing a doorway into a dark shaft. Inez chirped at the guard and led the way inside. It wasn't much larger than a sleeping closet on a spaceship. Chico followed, holding his breath, expecting another turbulent ride through a wormhole. But this time the floor operated as a simple lift. They rode up in silence and with minimal pressure from their speed, up from the damp, while he counted the seconds in his head.

The lift bumped to a stop, a door slid open, and they stepped out onto a covered balcony overlooking the sea far below. A shoreline curved in the distance, almost to the horizon. The city of stone buildings looked like rubble from here. He stepped closer to the edge, while Inez chirped at more attendants awaiting them on this balcony. Leaning out over a waist-high railing, he caught a breeze in his face as he peered down from the sphinx's eyeballs.

"Time is wasting," Inez said, nudging him from behind. "Let's go."

4

Landon had only used the SLP sensor the day before, tracking the Tititri signal. And now it sat on the pedestal designed for an alien's head to rest in petrified repose. Where was the rest of his equipment? Dust ground into the plastic casings. Rust had chewed away the metal fixtures, leaving dangling pieces. His machine had almost been new the day before. This object before him was an antique replica of his device. How could that be?

He touched the worn edge of the box. "Goiás," he said slowly, "we've got a problem."

The machine crumbled into a pile of litter.

He sank to his knees and lowered his head.

The earpiece in his helmet crackled. "Landon? What did you say? What is it now?"

But he was too dazed to answer Doc. He pulled himself up and turned away from the rubble. Slowly, he continued past more pedestals. They looked like children, these people. One of them stood out, being significantly larger, as large as a human. He paused to examine its contours more closely. Hands arranged across the alien's breast. Fingers tucked into fists. Then he noticed a thumb, a tiny thumb, poking between two fingers.

It was a *figa*.

Inez! Inez had been here. She'd fallen through a gate of some sort, and a time portal had brought her safely into the distant past, when the Tititri lived. She'd lived with them.

Doc spoke quickly in his earpiece. "Landon, I have been thinking."

Inez and her *figa* had influenced this petrified alien. No, it was larger. Large enough—

"Don't touch a thing," Doc said softly. "Not one thing, you understand me? We don't know what killed those people. It could've been a virus, and it might be dormant..."

She continued with her clinical instructions, but Landon wasn't paying attention to her. Could it be? Maybe this being that he touched was Inez herself.

Sobs shuddered through him. Molly... Inez... All of his losses sharpened in this instant. He fell across the petrified body—either it was Inez or else it was someone who'd known her. The icy stillness of death seeped through him.

He felt alone in the dark with floating patterns of dust. The cold dark.

He couldn't move. A chill gripped him. He shivered, spasming out of control, until he thought his teeth would rattle.

He hunched his shoulders, but it didn't stop the torment of cold. Tears welled in the corners of his eyes, and he wanted to abandon this place. More than anything, he wished he'd not taken that first step that had ultimately led him into this chamber of ice.

Then he wondered—irrelevantly—if his suit corder was picking up any of this. It would be proof of this madness. But it hadn't recorded Inez's accident. Probably because of the energy disturbance from that gate. Was there a disturbance down here? He glanced around. His skin prickled.

"All *right*!" Doc shouted, her words finally penetrating Landon. "If you don't talk to me, then I'm coming in there. Right now."

Frozen in time, these people were preserved as rock until the end of time itself. It had ended this way for her, but it didn't have to end this way forever.

"Landon, do you hear me?"

He pulled away from the ice-smooth form of the body preserved from death. Straightened. Squared his shoulders. "Yeah, I hear you. Stay there. I'm coming for you."

If Inez had traveled through the time portal, then so could someone else. If different points in time co-existed, then Inez and Chico were still alive in one of them. It would be a better plan to find that portal rather than the relic of his tachcom.

Landon stood up and surveyed the cavern full of alien bodies. They'd taken Inez into their midst. She'd lived out the rest of her life—and perhaps Chico, too—with aliens. One day, their descendants—a blend of human and Tititri—would return here with the technology to revivify these remains.

It wasn't much hope, but it was the best chance they had,

without a spaceship to take them home. They didn't even have a rover to carry them back to base and their cryo-tanks.

He had to find that gateway. And he had to maneuver himself, Doc, and Ruy into it.

"We'll be back," he murmured to the petrified Tititri, and then he turned to retrace his footprints to the exit.

Something moved in the air around him, something that wasn't dust or the light of his helmet. A soft, bluish violet light, growing stronger now, moving toward him. He stumbled backwards, watching the spot of color grow larger in the dark, descending on him. Then it split apart, as if an invisible knife had sliced through the fog. Two glowing figures stepped out from the parted slice. One tall, one short.

Tingles of recognition fired through him. "Molly?"

He staggered at first, wavering with uncertainty. And then he knew. Pushing through his momentary paralysis, he ran toward them. It was his baby girl. He'd know her anywhere. But he didn't recognize the person who was with her. Whoever it was, this person had apparently and inexplicably rescued Molly from the fires of Proxima.

5

Chico felt like the sphinx itself, surveying its domain from the vantage point of its eyeball. He knew its riddle—why was the sphinx both a terminal and a healer? He didn't know, but he probably should. He'd traveled through its terminal via a transporter that Queenie controlled, and he'd also experienced the healing powers of the egg cradles that her sphinx had produced.

He couldn't wait to meet her. He turned away from the balcony's rail and followed Inez into a chamber that filled the interior of the sphinx's head. At first he didn't see the number one alien for all the clutter of the room, dappled with rainbow colors. Tapestries and rugs padded the walls and floors of the stone structure. Cushions piled into stacks, and curtains—of woven cloth, not smoke—draped the corners.

Song chatter damped and muted from all the padding, and then he saw her. She nestled in cushions. The tawny amber flesh of her face camouflaged against swirls of the same colors behind her. A cape, the shade of a fine port, covered her, and she melted into her background, hidden from his examination. Was she even a she? Whatever she was, her size looked too small to impress him. She didn't look so queenly, but then, he'd never met a queen before.

Inez ignored his fidgets and called to the queen with twittering sounds.

That's when he noticed her eyes. They shone a shade of green so green it almost looked fake, like a stagnant lake. Queenie and Inez chirped some more while he remembered some of the women he'd known who'd enhanced the color of their eyes. Really, stagnant lake green wasn't so unusual.

But he didn't like the way these two chatty women seemed to have forgotten his presence. He'd thought the queen needed him.

"Relax, Chico," Inez said. "She's telling me about the water."

"What water?"

"Exactly. What you see out there is the last of their water, thanks to the Zyvors. Soon, Titra will become uninhabitable. They are in urgent need of finding a new home."

"And they want me to build them a spaceship? Tell her I just fly them. She needs someone else. Can we go home now?"

"There is not enough time for conventional flight. They have another plan. They will use the last of the water to flood themselves. Petrifaction will be a means of preservation for their bodies, while their genetic code implants on new bodies in another place."

"What place?"

"A safe place. They've been studying the cosmos to find such a place. Have you forgotten their observatory already?"

Earth. They were watching Earth. A chill ran through him.

Inez went on. "In a way, it's rather like our cryo-tanks, don't you think?"

"Except that it won't work."

"You sound just like Landon," she said with a laugh. "He thought he was always right, too. We had a conversation about all this, he and I, and I know I was right. I am sure of it. Yes, the signal from the sphinx is what brought us here, to this planet, but it's more than that. Petrifaction is the ultimate means of communication across time itself."

He snorted. "Landon works too hard. Me, I'm nothing like that."

"You'd better hope that some of him has rubbed off on you, if you truly want to get home. You remember your basic training in the use of his tachcom?"

"Yeah? What about it?"

"He was working on a remote unit, assembling it on our very first expedition into the sphinx's mouth. That's when we found the wormhole, or rather, the wormhole found us. Anyway, his machine came through with me, and that's why the Tititri modified my code—"

"They *what*?"

"At least, that's what I think they did. It happened in my healing egg—"

"And you *let* them?" He was aware of Queenie in her cushions, smirking at their exchange. Screw her.

"Settle down, Chico. I had to learn to communicate with them, you see? They gave me that ability while I healed from my fall."

He shook. He wasn't sure if it was from rage or fear. "Why didn't they teach *me* their bird talk while they had me strapped down?"

"No need. They have me for translation purposes. They wanted to learn something else from you. How to use the tachcom to transport genetic code as blueprints."

"Shit."

"They already have the ability to make the blueprints." She strode across the room and lifted one of the tapestries to reveal an egg cradle. "They can do that in these. But now they need a device to send those blueprints across space and time. They need Landon's tachcom. They tried to bring him here, but he resisted their efforts."

Chico's chest swelled. Sure, he knew the basics about Landon's machine. It made sense that they'd caught him in their wormhole and brought him here. Wait, had he just thought that?

"In the absence of Landon," Inez said, "they want to learn from *you*."

She swished aside a curtain that covered a niche in the stone wall. He recognized the scoop that hooked into a blinking display—it was Landon's tachcom. Wires sprung from this machine, connecting it to the egg cradle. Chico felt his jaw gape.

Inez continued, her words hammering into his head. "They need to master the use of the tachcom in order to send the blueprints of their genetic code. They will experiment by sending us, in exchange for what you can teach them. All I knew how to do was to send a message to Earth. Which I did. It's the message that started our entire mission. We seem to be caught in some sort of time loop."

"This is nuts," he finally managed to say, thinking aloud in a dazed state. "They don't need us. They need some crazy person instead...someone like that wack-o wife of Landon's. Summer."

A chirping song twittered from the cushions where Queenie lay. Inez exchanged a few more trills, and then spoke again like a normal person. "The Tititri blueprints will implant on new bodies that they grow, but there is a complication."

"What could possibly go wrong?"

"Rebels."

It had been a rhetorical question. He hadn't expected an answer. "What rebels?"

"Not everyone here agrees with the Titinha's wishes. Some Tititri have splintered away from the mainstream. They are rebels, and they think that instead of building new bodies from their genetic code, they should just claim a host body instead."

He didn't like the sound of that. "Where do they think they can find host bodies?"

"On Earth."

187

Chapter Ten

Landon pitched forward, tripping over the rubble that littered the floor of the cavern deep inside the sphinx. He tumbled to his knees and stared up at the ghostly figures approaching him. Was that it? They were ghosts. His baby girl was a ghost.

She'd awakened aboard the *Centaurus* when the ship had been pulled into Proxima. She couldn't have survived that.

But he didn't believe in ghosts.

And these figures didn't glow a ghostly blue-violet anymore. They'd stepped out of the light.

"Dr. Walker," a steely voice said to him. It wasn't a question but a statement, and it sounded as if it came from inside his head, rather than through his earpiece that connected him to Doc. It was a woman's voice, and now he recognized her.

"Commander Masambwa! But you...the *Centaurus*... How...did you get here?" They wore no spacesuits. They couldn't survive in this airless, frozen environment. Maybe they really were ghosts.

"Landon?" Doc said through his earpiece. "Who are you talking to?"

"It's...it's Molly. She's here, and so is—"

"It was simple, really," Masambwa said, her voice dominating the mic in his suit. "We used the wormhole network, kindly

189

activated by your daughter's platform, while Zyvor bubble skins protect our bodies and keep us breathing. Now all this is mine."

"Da-a-a-a!" Molly cried.

The sound of his little girl's raw terror pierced through him. Impossibly, she and Masambwa were real. "Baby!" He lurched forward, springing from his knees.

"Landon," Doc said in his ear. "You need to return to me at once. You're suffering from hallucinations. They will overcome you without treatment. I have the drugs you need in my beltpac."

"Stay where you are, Dr. Walker." Masambwa curled her fingers together into a pincer claw and then latched onto a spot, hidden to him, at the back of Molly's head. "Or else I will de-activate the bubble that keeps the platform of your daughter alive."

His forward momentum froze in a heartbeat. His chin lowered, bumping against his helmet's transmitter. "Get Ruy down here," he mumbled to Doc. "On the double. I need...his help. Not your drugs."

"No one can help you now," Masambwa said with an evil sound that might've been a chuckle from another person. Not from her. The commander didn't know how to laugh. What mattered more was that she'd heard him just now.

A tidal wave of questions slammed through his mind. Why did his mission commander want to hurt any of them, especially Molly? Why did either of them still live? Why were they here? Why did they have Zyvor tech? He managed to say, "But... why?"

"Because," Masambwa said, "I cannot allow you to interfere. Human bodies are such a nuisance. They are too needy to be of much use in space."

It didn't sound like his commander. "Who are you? You're not...human." *It* was going to hurt his little girl. He wouldn't let it.

"Very good. You detect the truth of my hybrid status. You would call my original an activist Tititri whose genetic code implanted on this human body. While in transit, we intersected during the Jupiter project. The essence of the human who once owned this body still resides, although displaced, buried deeply within, leaving me in charge of the body's functions. It is not an ideal arrangement, but it is better than what the Titinha decided for our people. Now she will pay for that decision."

"No," he said, "you're the one who will pay." Nothing mattered except for his daughter. He couldn't help Masambwa. But he still had a chance to save his baby girl. "Let Molly go. She's just a child."

"She is the platform that hosts the Titinha."

He remembered the name. She was the woman whose face sometimes emerged from within Molly. The woman whose eyes changed Molly's to emerald green. She'd spoken to Landon once before, through Molly's lips in Patagonia, under the glacier where Summer, Molly's mother, lay dying.

"If you're still in there," he said, turning to his daughter, trying to address the alien inside. "Talk to me. Now. Help me." He'd wanted to suppress the alien, by inserting Molly into cryo-sleep, but now he realized that mistake. He needed the alien, so that Molly could survive. "Help us."

Molly's eyes rolled in her head. Illuminated under his helmet light, they glowed like green jewels. The child whimpered, but the alien remained quiet.

"She won't come out now," Masambwa said. "She's a

coward. She knows I'll take her power if she shows."

"What power can she possibly have?" Landon said. "In a child?" He forced confidence into his voice, but a tremble ran through his knees. He remembered the way Molly had babbled to voices in her head and then made things happen. Was that the power Masambwa was talking about? He'd tried to suppress that, too.

There was no need to suppress anything any longer. The voyage was over now.

"Not the child," Masambwa said. "Of course she's helpless. But the Titinha is not. The Titinha controls the nexus of the wormhole network. That's how she activated the one that brought us here from the *Centaurus*, after I'd prepared the ship."

"Sabotage," Landon said. "You mean that you sabotaged the ship. What else did you do besides tampering with my instruments?"

"It was the only way to acquire the power. Why else do you think I allowed your daughter along on the mission? Now she is going to lead me to the source. It is here. Here, within the ark. Can you feel it?" Masambwa's rail-thin body jerked, as if she tightened her grip on the back of Molly's head. Molly choked and gasped, sucking pitifully at air.

"Don't hurt her!" Landon sprang forward, twisting the oxygen tank attached to his suit, wrestling to free it from its connections. He wouldn't hesitate to thrust its tubing into Molly's throat at his own cost. He would give his daughter the last of his air.

But as he closed in on Molly, a flash of movement plucked the canister of oxygen from him. Masambwa waved her free arm and held the canister in a defiant power gesture above her head. Her other hand tightened its grip on the back of Molly's neck.

A red light flashed inside his helmet. He opened his mouth to scream his protest, but only a gurgling sound came out. Molly's eyes widened, blazing green.

A new voice thundered from the dark. "No!" It was the Titinha, speaking in her deep, throaty voice that resonated from Molly's lips. "You have betrayed enough of our people. You must not hurt these innocents. You will let them live, and I will show you what you seek."

Through the black dots that swam across Landon's vision, he could see Masambwa smirk. She—or *it*—loosened its grip on Molly. His baby girl with the blinking green eyes breathed a sigh and pulled away from the hybrid activist who'd stolen Masambwa's body. The child turned on her heels and ran away into the dark. Masambwa tossed the oxygen canister at Landon and darted after Molly.

As he sucked life back into his lungs, Ruy's voice spoke through his earpiece. "Landon? What is this place? Where are you? I can't see anything but footprints in the dust."

"Good. Follow them, and you'll catch up to me. I'm going after them." He reattached the canister and took off.

"After who? I am supporting Doc, who is able to hop on one leg. We can't make it very far like this."

"You'll do it. You have to. This is the only way out."

"Are you sure? I do not see an exit. But luckily, I left a cable attached to our excavations above, and so we should—"

"Forget that. There's another way out of here." And he

would find it. But he didn't tell Ruy that he wasn't sure yet if it even existed.

Ruy continued a steady stream of questions and complaints, but Landon tuned them out. He couldn't let Molly—or the Titinha guiding his baby girl—vanish from his sight.

But they had disappeared already. He shone his light around himself in despair. Petrified aliens lay quietly in their shell-like pallets. All that he saw was disturbed dust. Their prints headed deeper into the sphinx, and he followed their trail. He hoped Ruy and Doc weren't too far behind him.

"Hurry!" he said into his helmet mic.

Heavy, gulping breaths rasped back at him, and he wasn't sure if the sounds were his own or from his teammates behind him, or maybe his daughter ahead. He doubted if the thing controlling Masambwa even needed to breathe. It wasn't human any longer. It was a hybrid, Masambwa's voice had said, a fusion of alien and human. Landon shuddered. Was that the future of Earth? His own future would shortly run out.

No.

No, it would not. He would make it back to Earth, where he and his daughter would have a future. He would make the Titinha release Molly. He wouldn't let Masambwa's hybrid have her.

He stumbled past endless rows of petrified aliens, until their prints finally led to an opening in the wall. Spinning round and round, he felt light-headed. Was his oxygen already running out? He didn't know, since the status light had not reset to green when he'd reattached the canister. The color red strobed with a steady pulse in his head. Yet, he still breathed. With so much left to do...

He staggered and felt himself drop into a pit.

It was only a short fall. The light gravity gave him a floating sensation, and then he landed softly upright and balanced on the balls of his feet. Jarred, but nothing felt broken. He'd left his prints up there, above his head, ending at the edge of the pit. The same fall would be less kind on Ruy and Doc, with her broken ankle.

"Ruy," he said with a gasp as he peered up into the darkness overhead. He did not see the light from his helmet, not yet. "Doc. Do you hear me? Watch yourselves. There's a hole, and I fell into it. Search for another way down."

Down here, where he had fallen, he glimpsed a spot of purple piercing the darkness. He tried to shine his light on it, but it wasn't solid, and the color wouldn't hold still. Particulates waved sinuously like a ribbon of fog through the dark. A purple cloud had swallowed Inez. An anomaly. Was this it? The entrance to the time rift that had taken Inez?

Masambwa's voice boomed out of the darkness surrounding the anomaly. "Where is it?"

Molly sobbed. The swirling purple cloud carried his daughter's wails, and their sound echoed throughout the pit, hammering inside Landon's head.

He charged forward, shouting. "Let go of her!"

"Stay back," Masambwa said, "or the girl dies now."

The Titinha's steady voice responded with equal steeliness. "You will not hurt her before you get what you want."

Masambwa: "This is not the nexus. It's just the entrance to another wormhole."

The Titinha: "It is the transporter that you want. It will

take you to our new world. Earth. You should not have left it to return here."

Masambwa: "I had no choice! It was the only way to take possession of the nexus."

The Titinha: "It is not for you to take. Would you destroy all the knowledge that we have acquired over the millennia?"

Their words fired back and forth, ringing inside Landon's head. He stumbled, swaying on his feet. The past swam through his mind.

The tachyonic emission he'd collected... It seemed an eternity ago, back when he still worked on SpaceHab, where Molly had been born. That emission must have been the signature of Tititri movement through wormholes.

The emission had contained a message... *Don't come.* Even then, the Titinha was trying to warn them away from here. She was trying to prevent this very moment from happening.

"You don't know what I want," the rebel alien screamed from within Masambwa, its voice cracking. "I want the nexus! Where is the nexus?"

"It is here," said the Titinha with controlled calm. "Inside me. It is that which directs the network. It is me."

"Give it to me now, or the girl dies, and then you will have nowhere to hide."

Landon's heart jolted in his chest. "Listen to it! Give it what it wants. Whatever that nexus is that Masambwa wants, it's no good to you anymore."

"It is what makes me who I am," the Titinha said. "The leader of our people is always grown as keeper of the nexus. It is safe within me. It will not transfer."

"That's a lie!" Masambwa screamed.

The Titinha continued patiently. "It cannot be transferred to any other Tititri, and certainly not to a rogue—"

Masambwa howled. "You're not my leader! When my cell broke into the network the first time, we found strong bodies, albeit human. And I got the best one of all. Mine enabled me to return here, to the source of the power. I speak for all of my cell. You'll never destroy us."

"You are nothing but a rogue," the Titinha said, "who has done the unforgivable by compromising the body of one of Earth's native peoples."

"If you really believe that," Landon said, "then you are guilty of the same thing. Get the hell away from my daughter!"

The Titinha gave a soft sigh of exasperation. "You cannot help yourself for not understanding our ways. Your child is not compromised with my presence. It's not the same as the way rogues take over their hosts. For the majority of us, a human host nurtures our transition, and then we emerge. Please, you must trust me—"

Masambwa snorted. "Who can trust you? Look at you, stuck inside a child's body. Not even you, the great leader of the Tititri, planned it to happen this way."

The sense of calm that had controlled the Titinha's voice now wavered. "The rogue is right. We made a mistake. But Landon, you must believe me."

He didn't know that aliens could make mistakes, too. As he himself had done, too many times to count. His mistakes had led to the breakup of his marriage, and all that had snowballed, eventually bringing him here.

If she was capable of mistake, then yes, maybe he could believe her. Understanding shuddered through Landon. The

Tititri didn't want to destroy Earth. Nor take it over. They were trying to adapt. They were trying to survive a death sentence, imposed by their enemies, the Zyvor.

"The mistake we made," the Titinha said, "was made in innocence. The human you sent to us, the one who fell through the time rift, guided me to a host for my transition to the new world. We did not know that she was 'pregnant'."

"You mean Summer? Then, Chico told you about her. That's how you ended up inside Molly. It was Summer all along that you aimed for."

Gasps clamored in Landon's earpiece, strongly enough that he thought at first it was his own breath sucking out of his lungs. Then he saw a narrow lightbeam, dancing in the dark from Ruy's helmet as he approached, holding up Doc.

"Holy shit!" Ruy cried.

Doc swore a stream of French.

Ruy went on muttering. "What the hell is this place?"

They flung their questions back and forth while Masambwa stepped away from them and closer to Molly. Green eyes blinked with a child's innocence and a strong leader's patience.

Then the Titinha went on. "We Tititri are grown externally, in a device that your 'Chico' called an 'egg'. We do not reproduce in your internal way. We do not emerge until we are fully grown. Likewise, it would be fatal to emerge from your 'Molly' until she is full grown."

"Don't believe her," the rogue said through Masambwa. "She lies."

"Who are you?" Doc said. "You're not Commander Masambwa."

Masambwa attempted another non-human chuckle. "The

Titinha has always lied. She is selling our people to the Zyvors, and I am telling you that we will not go along with her deception any longer. Once we have control of the nexus, we will become greater than the Zyvors ever dreamed."

The Titinha continued, as if the rogue hadn't spoken or Doc and Ruy's arrival hadn't interrupted. "Once your daughter reaches maturity, my essence will be ready to release into a new body of my own, grown specifically for that purpose in Tititri laboratories at the bottom of your world, our new world. We have already spoken of this. Do you remember?"

Landon remembered. Patagonia.

"We wish only to integrate with Earth in peace," the Titinha said. "My people can give your people many gifts of our knowledge, and we will bring you peace."

"Take it, Landon," said Doc. "Sounds like a good deal."

"But wait," said Ruy. "What is the offer?"

"Your daughter will not be harmed during this transition, not as this rogue has done to your commander, and not as a few other rogues have also done. We will root them out and eliminate them in the name of peace. That is why we have come back here, to the remains of our ancient center of culture. It is to lure the rogues away from Earth."

Landon thought of Patagonia, where the Titinha had given him cryptic instructions. "You asked me to find the alignment in time. And this is it, isn't it? So I found it. This purple cloud. What do we do now? Or have we arrived too late?"

"It is not a question of timeliness but rather of dimension. You have called it a rift in time. When the fabric of space-time folds in such a way that our systems align, the network opens. That's all the nexus is. That's when our genetic reading can pass through. With the arrival of your machine through the time rift to the final days of Titra, we gained your knowledge and used it to combine with ours in order to control the network. Your people helped me learn to set up the time loop."

"Chico?" Ruy said. "And Inez?"

"They're alive?" said Doc.

The Titinha went on. "And you, Landon, with your special skills, you know how to finish the job. With your special help, we will rescue the rest of our people and complete their transmission to the new world. That's why you had to come here. Your mission had to happen to make the time rift occur."

"You don't see its potential," Masambwa said. "We can use the nexus to rise throughout the galaxy. We will become more powerful even than the Zyvor."

"Go ahead," said the Titinha. "I invite you to step into the network."

Masambwa stepped closer. "Why should I do as you say? You're trying to trick me."

"It will take you to our new world, where we will all be safe from the Zyvors. All of us, together, including the rogues."

"Just give me the key to the power, and I'll decide where I go with it." Masambwa dove toward Molly, but the little girl sidestepped out of the commander's reach.

Molly yelped in her baby voice, and Landon leapt toward Masambwa. He'd practiced the blitz technique with his martial arts many times, and luckily Masambwa didn't know how to use it against him. His punch caught her in the chest, knocking the breath out of her and sliding her backwards nearly a meter farther away from the swirling purple cloud. He hated hitting a woman, even more than the dreaded act of striking a superior officer, but he reminded himself who she really was. Neither a woman nor his commanding officer. Besides, the purple cloud was the entrance to the Titinha's transporter, and it would take them home. He had to protect it from the rogue alien using Masambwa.

"Go, Ruy!" Landon shouted. "Now! Take Doc, and jump into the center of the purple cloud. It's a wormhole connecting us to Earth."

Ruy had apparently seen enough to make him understand to move without questions for once in his life. He and Doc sprang for the entrance, and tendrils of purple wrapped around their spacesuited figures. They disappeared from sight.

"You can't..." Masambwa said, sputtering, "stop me." Holding her bruised ribs, she rolled onto her side and pushed herself up onto her knees.

Landon grabbed Molly and lunged across the cavern, toward the spot of purple where his teammates had stood only seconds ago.

Masambwa bellowed behind him. Pain—or the alien that had taken over her body—distorted her words. "Can't...stop *us!*"

He squeezed Molly tightly against his chest and tripped against a low rim encasing the purple sphere.

Words roared around him. "There are others!" Human-alien words exploded with the fuel of star power. "Others of my kind on Earth!"

Sliding sideways, Landon thought his momentum was going to carry him and Molly through the purple cloud and out the other side. He thought the wormhole had closed behind Ruy's and Doc's passage. He thought—

Silky warm, invisible arms cradled him. The floor dropped

beneath his feet. The air ripped and spiraled above them, swallowing them. Molly tipped her head back. Her tiny thumb poked against his chest, and her green eyes blinked upwards. In response to her gaze, the ragged edges of the rip knitted together, closing the wormhole behind their passage. No one could follow them now.

Epilogue

A scorching sun beat down on Landon's head as soon as he pushed through the exit of the administration building where the press conference was wrapping up. He clutched Molly's hand, pulling her along behind him. She didn't seem to mind. She was singing, either a song of nonsense syllables to herself or else she was carrying on a conversation with the Titinha.

Outside, heat and bright light slapped him face on. He squinted and sucked in long and slow, a deep breath of Brazilian air, tasting the red dust of this man-made desert here in Goiás. He was grateful not to wear a helmet and that no red light pulsed its warning message at him.

He was grateful for a lot of things, starting with the wormhole that had brought him home.

And especially Molly. The Titinha had kept his baby girl safe. Himself and the others, too. All except for Masambwa and Brandt. They hadn't made it back.

Footsteps clattered behind them on the cement walkway connecting the white buildings of the International Space Agency's compound. "Landie!" his sister Greer called to him. "Wait up."

He grimaced at the old nickname, but considering the way she glowed in his presence, now that he'd returned to Earth, he let it slip by. Her smooth flesh, free of puffs and wrinkles, was painted with an artist's touch, making her look ten years younger than the image of her that he'd seen on the message she'd transmitted across space.

"Where are you going?" she said, catching up to them. "The reporters want to talk to you."

"Chico can handle them for me." The pilot was doing a fine job back there, basking in the glory of attention from the press. "You want to come along and help us check out my new quarters?"

Greer took Molly's other hand and continued chattering over the top of the little girl's reddish golden curls, so like her mother's. "I never thought I'd see the day that you admitted I was right. And not just to me, but to the entire world, the way you did back there just now. I knew all along about those aliens being here. Didn't I try to tell you?"

He started to correct her but then thought better of it and smiled. Let her think the press conference had been all about her. What could it hurt? It had been Sam's idea to invite the press here. It was time, the ISA director had said—especially considering the leaks that Greer had initiated—time to confirm the news of the alien presence among humanity. The Titinha had accepted this inevitability, in light of the crew's return to Earth without a spaceship. The official story was that the Tititri had helped humans and would continue doing so. With one condition: that the alien leader's presence in Molly remain a secret.

Okay. He accepted that, too, considering how she'd gotten them out of the sphinx and safely home.

"You're looking good, Greer," he said as they strolled. Molly skipped between them. "No more near accidents? No one chasing you anymore?"

Her laughter tinkled and her powdered cheeks glowed. "Oh, that. It's all over now, those alien wars. The good aliens won, don't you know? You were there."

He grunted in semi-acknowledgement. Was that what it was, his struggle with that rogue who'd stolen Masambwa's body? A *war*? Their commander and Brandt had been the casualties. But he didn't feel as confident as his sister that it was over. What would happen, once the Zyvors discovered where the Tititri were hiding?

"You must know," she said with an irritated sigh. "The rebels have no reason to stalk me anymore, now that the queen's troops won. That's what Chico told me when he and Inez returned. And the queen herself closed the box drawers after the rest of you used them to return. That's what he said she said."

He understood now that she was talking about the Tititri network of wormholes. "He told you all that?"

"Don't be so smug, Landie. I'm not stupid, you know."

"I never said you were." He smiled. Some things never changed.

Greer harrumphed and went on. "Well, because you and Molly *are* back, I don't want to miss out on another single day. You *are* staying on Earth this time, aren't you? It sounded like that's the plan, what you told those reporters just now."

"Speaking of which," he said, "ISA offered me a cottage here in the compound, and—"

"You'd have to give up your precious lab on SpaceHab."

"Not entirely. Jackson has been running it without me for a long time now. I would travel up there from time to time to consult on matters."

She shook her head. "Won't you ever learn? The courts gave me custody long ago, remember?" She blinked down at Molly, who seemed unaware of them as she sang her nonsense song.

He let out a low growl. "I'm trying to ask if you'll stay here with us. Molly will need both of us." Besides, the arrangement would put him closer to Inez, here in her native land.

"Oh, Landie," she said, grinning. "I thought you'd never ask."

As they continued toward the residential sector, he tried to listen to his daughter's lyrics in spite of the way Greer babbled on. He was pretty sure the song Molly sang was to herself and not a conversation with the Titinha. The emerald eyes had faded back to their normal hazel ever since the wormhole had emptied them out in a portal, deep within a piece of jungle—one of the secrets left in the Amazonian rainforest.

He accepted the alien's presence now. He knew she wasn't going to hurt his daughter. She'd promised she would leave his daughter's body once Molly grew to maturity, and after all they'd been through together, he believed her. Anyway, it wasn't just about the two of them anymore. All of humanity was going to need the Titinha's help in the days ahead, as Earth took in alien refugees.

"Dr. Walker?" said a voice behind them.

Releasing Molly's hand, he turned and squinted into the sun. It was Sam Talcott, his bear shape in a white suit jiggling as he hurried to catch up. He'd let his hair grow long as a lion's mane, completely gray now, and it flapped behind him. A couple of journalists followed. Landon flinched, reminded of an image of H.F. For a moment he thought he'd been caught in a time warp. Or else the remains of his old mentor had been restored.

No. It was Sam—former astronaut who'd piloted with Masambwa on the Jupiter project—famous Sam and not H.F., who directed ISA now.

"Dr. Walker," Sam said, extending his right arm. A touch of gold gleamed between his fingers. "You missed the presentation at the end. I believe this medal is yours."

Greer squealed, and Landon shoved his hands into his trouser pockets. He didn't deserve a medal. He'd only been doing what any parent would do, trying to keep his daughter safe. He'd done that, despite the high cost. They'd lost two of the crew and the ship, best of the fleet.

Sam shrugged and passed the medal to Greer. "You keep it for Molly, then."

"Oh, I will," Greer said. "I'll make sure she understands one day, just how precious this is."

Cameras flashed, capturing the moment.

"Dr. Walker," shouted one of the journalists, "when are you going to Patagonia?"

Landon shrugged. "You'll have to ask Director Talcott about that."

"I think it can be arranged," Sam said with a chuckle, "now that aliens have been removed from the terrorist watch list. So far our excavations haven't found anything down there, but with Dr. Walker's help, maybe our crew will know more precisely where to look."

It wasn't likely. Summer's body—and the alien spaceship where Molly's mother had died—had probably shifted under that glacier into another wormhole. On purpose? The aliens knew how to manipulate wormholes. He wondered where they all were now, including the rogue holding Masambwa's body hostage. Had they reunited somewhere in Zyvor territory, via another wormhole?

It wasn't Landon's problem anymore. He had a daughter to raise. He smiled for the camera and shook Sam's hand. The ex-astronaut smiled back, his eyes twinkling with flecks of emerald green.

* * * * *

Rebecca S.W. Bates

Rebecca S.W. Bates writes speculative fiction. She lives in Boulder, Colorado where she raised three daughters and taught Spanish. Now she writes full time and enjoys traveling as much as possible. Her previous novels *The Signal* and *Prelude to Proxima* are both available from D.M. Kreg Publishing in ebook and trade paper format.

Her latest short story publications appear in the Fiction River anthologies Universe Between and Fantasy Adrift. Her science fiction and fantasy short stories have also appeared in Alien Aberrations, Infradead, Sorcerous Signals, Future Syndicate, Ecotastrophe, and the Colorado Book Award nominated Broken Links, Mended Lives. She has contributed several short science fiction stories to *Tough Mothers* and *The Time Is Light* and fantasy stories to *Three Goofy Stories*. See first chapters and her collections of short stories at www.dmkregpublishing.com.

www.ingramcontent.com/pod-product-compliance
Lightning Source LLC
Chambersburg PA
CBHW070010260626
47159CB00005B/1741